Borrowed Lives

SUNY Series,
The Margins of Literature

Mihai I. Spariosu, Editor

Borrowed Lives

Stanley Corngold
and
Irene Giersing

STATE UNIVERSITY OF NEW YORK PRESS

Production by Ruth East
Marketing by Dana E. Yanulavich

Published by
State University of New York Press, Albany

For information, address the State University of New York Press,
State University Plaza, Albany, NY 12246

Library of Congress Cataloging-in-Publication Data

Corngold, Stanley.
    Borrowed lives / Stanley Corngold and Irene Giersing.
        p. cm. — (SUNY series, the margins of literature)
    ISBN 0-7914-0671-7 (alk. paper). — ISBN 0-7914-0672-5 (pbk.:
alk. paper)
    I. Giersing, Irene (Date). II. Title. III. Series: SUNY
series, margins of literature.
PS3553.O674B67 1991
813'.54—dc20   90-44138
                                                                    CIP

10 9 8 7 6 5 4 3 2 1

This is a work of fiction. Any representation of persons living or dead is therefore rigorously unreliable.

Chapter One

A patch of light glinted through the trees. She ran toward it to see if it was fire, but there was no smell of smoke, and then she could not see the light anywhere again. The Candover Valley lay wide open below her, the lines of soft farming land and old brick villages smudged by the early mist. A buzzard coasted on the wind that drove scudding clouds above the hills.

She had had the dream again. Ever since arriving from the Var, she'd been having it. She was in La Casaubade, and Robert was trying to open the door of her room. Suddenly he came in, all the light around him, and she was happy. But then she saw his angry expression and knew he was going to leave her. She had woken up shouting and with the yelping of the carpenter's dog had never properly got back to sleep.

At a sudden crack in the thicket hedge she startled; a pheasant lurched up, wings beating wildly, and swooped off above the clearing. She watched its clumsy flight and saw, above them all, another sky rise up, in which the sun burned and the mistral howled.

Turning rapidly, she walked down the hill through the clump of woods to the cottage. Soon she would not be watching and waiting anymore. With the months gone by, and no news from France, she must be out of danger, no longer an exile in the bush. She was an émigré, biding her time and

1

waiting for peace to settle in her home. On passing the last copse she stopped at the sight of the green, mosslike lawn— tended for centuries by salaried handwork and cold rains—and the low, timbered house with its gray thatch reaching almost to the ground. At the side the daffodils were blooming; she wished she could love them more. The crunch of a bicycle on the gravel roused her, and she went around the house.

"Morning, Mrs. Stevens. Just come back from your walk? Mr. Bacon says to tell you he'll be late this morning." The postman handed her a bunch of envelopes.

She smiled and took them in. Discarding bills and *The Independent*, she tore open a letter from her broker—the usual warning against long-term bonds—then, grabbing a paring knife, slit open the remaining envelope.

The Apthorp, Apt. 11J
Broadway and 79th Street
New York, N.Y. 10024
March 28

Ms. Margot Stevens
Booker Cottage
Upper Wield
Hampshire, England

Dear Ms. Stevens:

I am writing in response to your advertisement in *The New York Review of Books* about a house for rent in the Var. I am a professor of history on sabbatical leave during the next academic year—unmarried, without children and pets—and do not antic- ipate visitors. I want to bring a lot of books: I have several projects and a craving for quiet and a splendid view.

Could you furnish me with further details and perhaps a few photographs?

I hope to hear from you soon.

Sincerely,
Paul van Pein

A history professor, she mused, like Karol, her last—at forty-nine "gone down for the long count," Robert had said.

He'd brought it on himself, probably: too many deadlines, too many all-nighters with double Armagnacs. Well, this lonely academic might do, might do nicely. She abhorred the thought of La Casaubade as a moratorium year for squabbling couples with scrambling children and carloads of friends coming up. Paul van Pein—a solitary academic. A penitent from those tense cloisters could very well serve.

As she absent-mindedly twisted the knife, her thoughts returned to La Casaubade, and the dismal picture came up again: walls crumbling, paint peeling, the windows and door-frames cracked by the wind. A proxy would have to be sent quickly to stave off the gray that was scumbling the lines in her mind. But surely her fears were unwarranted. She had been away for only a few months: dilapidation and ruin couldn't have settled in so quickly; on instinct Nicholas would be looking after things. In Hampshire, certainly, the damp could get into your bones but not there under the sun and scorching wind.

The ring of the telephone startled her, and the knife slid into her thumb. "Fuck!" She sucked her cut and lifted the receiver to deflect her anger.

"Hello."

"Daisy Holford speaking. Are you Margot Stevens? I'm so glad to have found you in. I am sorry not to have been in touch sooner, but I've been away. I knew, of course, you'd rented Booker Cottage. How odd that none of the Bookers wanted it. . . . Well, you must be feeling cut off—"

"No, Lady Holford, I'm not."

"Yes, you may say that. But please come to tea. Today. A few friends will be stopping by. It will be so good for you to meet them."

Since Margot's arrival in January, she had spoken to no one except the postman, the carpenter, and the gardener, and that was how she wanted it. The cottage had been rented for her by Karol's son, who had attended survival school with the younger Bookers. She knew county society, and she didn't want it, so it was with some surprise that she heard herself say, "I'd like to come."

She put the telephone back in the cradle. Whatever possessed me? I'm here to be alone, to keep to my circle.

On the deep green Mr. Bacon was on all fours, supposed to be clipping hedges. The smoothness of the lawn offended her—too different from the real thing: her scraggy gorse, jagged hills, and stony olive trees. It flattened the exhilaration she'd had on reading the letter. But solitude had taught her to leave such moods alone. Another would return—the mood of hope that grew on discipline.

The sky was darkening. She went into the garden, where the air had turned cool and foggy. The black soil cold between her fingers—knees damp, back aching—she planted seedlings for hours, row on row. The Candovers were purgatory, her work these past months redemptive. It had emptied her passions and hardened her will: she meant to be still firmer and more rigorous. Professor van Pein would have a letter from her that night. Only when the light began to fade, she stretched—stiff and cold—and went over to the gardener. "Be careful of your spine, Mr. Bacon," she said. "You ought to go home now."

In the bathtub, balancing a cup of whisky-laced tea, she considered her new prospect: she had had to leave La Casaubade, but she would not lose her place entirely. Now it would be someone else's to mind for her, but she would be right there beside him. He would be her eyes. Was it madness to identify her hideaway by sending a proxy? Robert could harass her in Hampshire if he wanted. But it was better to take the risk than go on living without news of him. Suddenly she laughed out loud, joyous. She had a plan. She would find out all about Robert and Catherine.

In the small bedroom with its timbers and slanting walls, she pulled on a leather skirt, high boots, and batik jacket and swept up her startling hair. But as the comb dug into a knot, she found herself combing through softer, darker curls, and hearing Catarina complain, "Don't," with a three-year-old's anguish, her eyes glassy with tears. That had been a lifetime ago: she had not often held her daughter since, and when Catarina had come to see her in France last summer, she had felt dismayed by how little connected them. She poured herself another whisky and threw on her cape.

How surprising the scene at the end of the room. After the cottage Holford House was lush. There were rich chintzes, dense Persian rugs, paintings of ancient Holfords in heavy frames, ginger jars on dainty tables, roses, deep sofas, and polished chairs against which stood people—rich people—chatting easily, dressed in silks and tweeds, well-coiffed, well-mannered, well-fed, well-spoken. It was half a lifetime since she'd been in such a room. Her hesitation didn't come from the fear of seeming uninformed: she was attuned and responsive to patterned social intercourse, like those who are so good at languages or musical instruments it seems they do not even have to learn the new ones. Yet she felt the tremor of an older wariness.

A middle-aged woman approached, her waved hair wound in a velvet band. "I'm Daisy Holford, Mrs. Stevens. I'm so pleased you could come. Do have some tea and meet my husband. May I call you Margot? It's such a lovely name."

Margot shook hands with a man who seemed a little rougher than the others, with a thick crest of gray hair and bushy black eyebrows. He looked like a warden of the Geographical Society, and that made him familiar, but she was not sorry when he handed her a cup of tea and steered her toward the Reverend Fervour, who with a Miss Salient was invoking the fabled beauty of the cobalt mango. Like her, both had seen the jungles of Vanuatu.

Partly to deflect their curiosity, Margot asked about the county. With his beard and domed brow, the vicar looked like one of the James family, a congener of Henry, William, or Alice not mentioned in the biographies. "There are fine examples of the thatcher's art in the villages," he said, "each pattern bearing the signature of the individual artisan. The porcelain cats crouching on the roofs are a reminder of the days when the house cat guarded the thatch from crows. But now the job is done by a carefully molded net casing." Margot felt something stir—the pleasure she took in accurate information. "Yes," said the vicar, smiling, "we've been Thatcherites for centuries here." She stared at him; he took a step back and said in a loud voice: "And you, Mrs. Stevens, where do you hail from originally?"

"From Boston, but the last few years I've been living in the South of France."

"How lucky you are," said Daisy Holford, coming up to her. "I have dear friends in Cannes."

"I rarely go to Cannes," said Margot. Margot abominated Cannes. "I live in the Var, in the first range of mountains in from the coast. It's too windy there for most tourists. The seasons are harsh, and the landscape is too stark."

"There I must disagree with you," said Robert Holford, looking intently at her. "I often hiked through the Gorges du Verdon as a young man. It's true the country is austere, even dangerous, but I found it invigorating."

She took a step directly into his gaze; she knew her eyes had turned a brilliant blue. "Yes," she said, "I know the hardness—but it can be excessive. I went to the Gorges to watch the eagles and stood in the middle of the bridge, thinking that if I allowed myself to lose concentration for a second, they would plunge down on me."

"My dear Margot," said her hostess, "whatever made you leave in the winter, leave all that sun behind?"

"Oh, just the feeling that it was time to go. I am lending the house to a friend." She smiled and moved across the room past a large mahogany trolley, heavy with silver and embroidery and rich food. She was drawn to the darkly varnished picture that hung above it: a woman in a torn dress, apparently of fur or hide, lay back in distress across a rock, her hair splayed out, while a shape in the corner—a large owlish head—peered harshly through the trees at her. In the foreground stood a fanciful palace or fortress. She squinted at the bottom to discover a legend: the picture wanted a moral motto, but she could not find one.

"You're a sight for a famished eye." The compliment came *sotto voce* from her left elbow. She turned and saw a florid, good-looking man in a too-tight jacket. "You mean the eager poacher," she said, handing him her cup and sandwich as she turned away.

"Wait a minute. That's a bit strong."

Margot shook his hand away and said quietly, with a smile, "Because I am strong," and then went to pay her respects to Robert Holford.

It was unlikely she would be harmed. She would be distracted, but she would not be got at. There had been rapidly murmured invitations from the vicar, from Miss Salient, and from the amorous Bramson-Pyne, of course. On the way out she had met Mrs. Bramson-Pyne, red-haired like her and still pretty, but worn with worry about her adolescent girls. She had asked Margot's advice and Margot had said: "Oh, leave them to themselves." So she had made a mark, with allusions to her traveled past and pseudoconfidences, but these were no longer overtures to another game. Repeated many times and rarely challenged, they'd become an empty ritual. And what to do about Morton Bramson-Pyne when the time came? Easy—that was his lookout. The point was dignity now and its element plain: solitude.

She was at the cottage, and as she saw its low silhouette, she felt that she could call up despair and it would come, but she would not do it. And after all, what could be easier to resist? There was a task at hand.

April 3

Dear Professor van Pein:

I was glad to receive your letter. I have always imagined that La Casaubade would be conducive to work of an academic nature.

The house is located in the hills to the north-west of Seillans. If you consult a good map, you will find it off the road connecting Draguignan and Grasse. La Casaubade is on a hill-top, commanding a view—you dreamt of one—which extends more than half-circle over vineyards, forests, and mountains. When the mistral is blowing, you can imagine you see the ocean to the south.

The property consists of three *berges*—terraces dug out to facilitate the cultivation of olive trees. There are as many figs and young apricots as olives now, which have been hard hit by a blight from Italy.

At the bottom of the *berges* are dense bushes full of black-berries and a fair amount of wild raspberries and asparagus. A small stony stream flows past them.

The house has a vegetable garden which you may want to keep up—there are two harvests a year, and the yield is abun-dant, but you will have to work hard. The walls of the house were once part of an eighteenth-century *mas* (farmhouse). Sever-al years ago, I redesigned the interior.

On the first floor is the living room, with a ceiling three stories high. The room has a large fireplace (there is ample wood for burning on the property), three double doors facing south, and a small window to the east. The floors are terra-cotta tile with Moroccan carpets. There are also wicker armchairs, woven by local craftsmen, oak tables with brass inlay, a leather sofa, and an old Zanzibar chest.

On the west side of the room is a plain refectory table and chairs: this is the dining room. Next to it is the kitchen—large and modern—with ash counters and cabinets, gas stove, refrigerator, and freezer.

From the kitchen, a winding stone staircase takes you past a landing to a study-cum-bedroom with a double bed, large desk and armchair, an old armoire, a chest, and Afghan carpet.

The staircase goes on up to the third floor. Here the ceilings are much lower and slope. The bedroom has a long window looking out over the the living room below. The bathroom, large and sunny, faces the valley to the west.

An addition stands in the back. It contains a workroom, with washing machine—the mistral will be your drier—and a storage room for gardening tools and machinery.

I hope you decide to take the house. It will give you good value, and the space now wants to be lived in.

Sincerely,
Margot Stevens.

She dozed into the raw sun and the purple heady air of the hills—hills full of rough, grayish grass, sage and spiky rosemary, brambles and gnarled pine trees, hills crazy from the sun and the wind.

She went to bed, dreamt, and woke.

She saw:
the jungle (heat bees sawtoothed plants mud);
    felt:
the month of nights strike into her stomach like a fist;
    heard:
the sneaky pad of naked feet nearing her hut and her heart racing.

She never knew if one of them would come or which one of them would come. Later there would be no recognitions, only dark faces that were darker in the night—and no words uttered, only odd murmurs, clicks, and stranger cries. At the best of times she felt a sense of familiarity, felt release, but then as the weeks passed, disgust blotted out everything but wanting still to feel their bodies strain against her in the endless dark.

On the margins of her consciousness, however, her curiosity had gone on working, because it was also a matter of pride to grasp the code that governed the order of uses—the order she'd penetrated by letting herself be used. Her curiosity saved her for a while, and then under the circumstances it seemed grotesque to think that what was at stake was thick description.

She ran away from Vanuatu. Years later, she found the ruin called La Casaubade and built it up, and on her hill in France lived well, yes, when she lived alone. But Robert had been there, and when she went back to him, she tried to think his thoughts, and that had not worked out at all.

How reckless to have wanted more, to have wanted him. And then to have taken up with Catherine! She'd talked too much to her, and their one embrace had been a gesture— theatrical, extravagant—above all, unnecessary. No, Robert could look her up in Hampshire if he wanted, but she would not go out to meet him—not until she had first turned things around. The news might be disastrous, but at least it would revoke the finality of their parting.

It had happened last fall.

The sky was turning bleak as she waited on the terrace, listening for the noise of his Mercedes bouncing up the hill. They would have the battle she had been expecting for days. But she was brushed by a wing of fear when she saw his face. He was coming up, in black sweater and black trousers, harsh as a crow against the rocks, his hands stiff against his sides.

"Where is she?"

Margot was silent.

"What did you do to her?"

"Don't start that way. I can't stand you that way. I haven't seen her for days."

"Don't lie." He took a step forward. "Just tell me what you did to her."

"I didn't do anything."

"Right. You didn't do anything, because she's nothing, except someone you use in your plots. Like Catarina."

She had to smash the look of hatred off his face. She drew her hand back and let it fly with all her strength and hit him. "I'm sorry, I'm sorry." She reached out to take his arm. "Robert, I don't understand. What's happened to Catherine?"

He was staring up at the house, holding his cheek. He turned and looked at her: "I don't know you."

"Don't say that." She began to cry, furious at crying.

"Your hands have been all over her. You're too free with your hands." He whispered, "Something terrible has happened."

"What are you talking about?"

"She might have killed herself."

"Are you sure?"

He nodded.

"You've seen her body?"

"How dare you ask me such a question?"

"How dare you withhold information? What does that mean, 'she might have killed herself'?"

Robert said, "She left me a letter, and now she's gone."

"And that proves it."

"I tell you, this time you're not going to get away with it."

"I suppose you had nothing to do with it. You should never have started anything with her."

"You made her do it because I wanted her."

"What did she write? Tell me her words, her actual words!" She was close to wailing, there on top of her sacred hill. But in the middle of the disgrace she'd stopped to look at him: he was exhausted, and for a second she wanted to hold on to him as he'd held her when the terror had struck. But he turned on his heel and walked down to the car. And she got scared. You thought you had a life and then suddenly it was smashed, and there were openings that could be walked into by anything and anyone. But now . . . there was a good thought stirring. Oh yes, this tenant, this little tenant, could be the means. Would be her proxy in this too. She clenched her fists, rolled onto her belly, and fell asleep.

Chapter Two

"This is perfect."

Paul was smiling the entire time as they followed the narrow road from Le Muy, moving inland off the bleak efficiency of the autoroute. The earth was red and rocky but full of scrub pines, ilex, and vines—sturdy and well-pruned, heavy with hard beginning grapes. "Wait a minute, stop. Jas d'Esclans. That's one of her places, the one with the good wine. We could get some now."

"That woman has possessed you," said Michael. He began to back up, shaking his head with feigned concern.

"It's in one of the letters." Paul rummaged through his briefcase and found it. "Good red wine here."

They turned into a long drive, flanked on both sides by clay urns full of greenery shining in the afternoon sun. A sturdy old woman in black hauled herself up from a straw chair—her cheeks stamped with the script of mornings and noons in blazing light and stinging wind. They asked for and got a case each of the vineyard's best red and white from the cool, dark storage room. To Paul's surprise the woman seemed displeased by their asking for her best, suggesting the next time they come, they bring a couple of plastic containers and get them filled with the wine everyone drank. At his mention of Madame Stevens, however, she brightened and said, "Ah oui, l'américaine. Une belle femme."

11

"What does that mean?" said Michael, as they drove back onto the highway, "A knockout, an upright being, or a correct bourgeoise?"

Paul shrugged. Now that they were almost there, he preferred to be alone. Michael was an old friend; he and Jane had never wavered as they saw him through his break with Nina. Paul had followed her to Hampstead and stayed with them in Pimlico, where one or the other was always ready to listen to him grapple with his loss. Jane reminded him of all the energy he'd have as soon as he got over Nina; and she and Michael had improvised a program of tasks and outings, encouraging him to spend his days at the Arts Center and read in the British Museum.

In Paris, he and Michael had stayed with Paul's cousin Léon—once a skirtchaser and now an eminent urologist. Michael had been busy with appointments of his own, so Paul was able to revisit the haunts of his adolescence where he'd dutifully obeyed *grand-mère*. After such long absence they emitted a heady freshness, ventilating the resentment he'd felt for the old woman who had ruined his summers with phonetic drills and guided tours of the mid-eighteenth-century sections of the Louvre. The buoyancy of Paris had fled in forced marches on squares and churches under the tutelage of beholden pedants. His grandmother's regime had later turned profitable, for he'd had an easy time with European history in college and graduate school; but then he'd also not been eager to stay in Paris, preferring Oxford, Vienna, and Florence for working visits. This had caused his grandmother chagrin, and Paul had had to accept with a shrug the designation of *ingrat*. Now, however, the house in the Var had drawn him matter-of-factly back, and he began to revisit his old stations, correcting the past with the present impression, unspoiled by resentment and vivified by contrast.

But his main purpose lay to the south, and promising Léon and Anne-Lise to return in the fall, he and Michael set off, driving through Burgundy—past vineyards and Romanesque churches—where they dined on rich stews, plump cheeses, and wines about a foot deep.

On the Rhône they met Lemarchand, a master chef elated that his restaurant had got a second star. "I know exactly what you're feeling," said Paul. "There are three ranks of university professors and three ranks of chefs. Promotion to associate professor means tenure—and if not wealth, then certainly economic security for life."

"You exaggerate."

"No," Paul said, "if you've got a second star, your performances are worth a detour, right? That will make you rich at least in the short run."

"With good reviews."

"Every bourgeois workplace is starting to feel like a university," said Paul, "the happy prison of self-promotion." At this, the chef produced some old rum, which they were unable to distinguish from the finest Armagnac, and charged them a fortune.

They spent an extraordinary night in the Ardèche. On the bare main street of a ghostly village parched by the mistral and under moonlight made of old bones, they picked up a couple of young Austrian women, seventh-semester students from the University of Innsbruck and punkers. Feeling invincible, Paul and Michael drank huge amounts of wine and put together incoherent conversations in German on writers whom the girls had never heard of. Mostly, they looked at each other and laughed, and Paul and Michael laughed with them. Together they danced an unrestrained *pas de quatre* through the empty streets of the wind-swept ruin, and on the hillside—Paul's heart beating as if it would break through his chest—they tumbled into the arms of the willing, though oblivious girls, making love as though there had never been a history of which Paul was a professor. It was, all in all—he thought in the car—an initiation rite to the South, a first and possibly last offering to the moloch of sensuality, something that was not going to be allowed at La Casaubade, where the point was renunciation and a husbanding and nurturing of resources for moral discovery.

From a letter Paul held in his hand, he began reading aloud instructions on how to spot the house. It was as if Margot had known and set down in advance every one of his reactions: excitement at the climb, impatience at the blocked views, expansion at the open vistas. "If this keeps up," said Paul, "I'll see the entire year through her eyes."

"What color are they, by the way?" said Michael.

"Purple—I don't know. She didn't want to meet." He paused. He was not sure whether to be glad or not. Before setting off from New York, he had proposed a meeting in London, where he would be staying with Michael and Jane for a week before driving to France, but her response had been surprisingly stern—no, she could not see any reason for meeting; it was unnecessary.

At the next exhilarating turn they would be at Nicholas and Jean's, where the keys had been left. "I'll wait here," said Michael, pulling the car over to one side of the richly planted driveway. He had been quiet during the last half-hour. Perhaps, with his great tact, he'd intuited and taken seriously Paul's mood of receptiveness to Margot alone, perhaps he partially shared it.

Paul walked down the sloping path to the house with its red-tiled roof, hidden among screw pines and hibiscus. On the door, tacked into the rough, sun-bleached wood, was a brown envelope with his name; inside were keys and a note. "Welcome to these heretical hills. Sorry, we're out for the day, so cannot greet you properly. All systems are ticking. Problems? Call us. N.V." It was a little jarring to find himself already known to these locals by name. He felt lucky not to have to meet them—new people, the wrong people in this scene where only Margot was really right. He hustled back up the drive, swinging the keys. "They're not home. I'll drive the rest of the way. Move over. You read," he said and showed Michael the right place in the letter.

"After Varda's house, the road gets rougher," Michael read, "so drive cautiously. The landscape will change abruptly as you come around the bend. Everything becomes sparser and less lush. There were fires some years ago, and although most of the burnt traces are gone, the general impression is one of savage bareness. The road will now begin to climb steeply, and at the top the view is suddenly liberated and overwhelms you from all sides. The house is at the bottom of a driveway which plunges down to the left. It's the only one, so you can't miss it—there's a mailbox without a name.

"I don't care for the angle of this driveway in winter," said

Michael. "There's the mailbox." It was on the ground, as if banged off at the base by a giant fist.

Paul stopped the car. "Well," Michael said, "your landlady promised you a view. She wasn't lying." They got out.

The house was built on the highest *berge*—massive, like an old donjon with walls of bleached ochre stone, broken in their rocky plainness by only a few clumps of fig trees, small oaks, and then an enormous chestnut. The terrace was covered with sun-whitened gravel with bunches of flowering herbs. Immediately in front of them, on the *berges* sloping down and away, it was true, the vegetation was low, scraggly, harsh—as much gray as green, with patches of scorched earth. But to one side, there was a rocky garden, and from its ledge the view sailed out over an immense distance, where green forested hills began, layer after layer, with rises like the *ensellure* of horses' backs. But the real view lay directly in front of them, on out past the once burnt ground. This was a marriage of earth and distance, rock and sun: far, far off, the mountain ridges glinted. There was no one in sight, no other houses, just purple mountains shining in the streaming light.

"The end of the world," said Paul.

"The beginning of yours. Jesus, what a find."

Paul unlocked the French doors leading from the terrace into the living room. The rugs were dark and brilliant, the woods polished, brass insignias gleamed from the old chest, the candlesticks shone, and the dusky gold of the stone walls, empty except for the old faded tapestry, soared up into the shadows.

Michael shook his head. "It's not like anything I've ever seen. Protestant and, well, sensual."

"You mean Catholic—old, Clunaic Catholic. What a place for work. To be equal to it all." Paul went upstairs. "I want to see the rest."

"The chapterhouse of the local furies," said Michael.

"Look at this view!" Paul went from the landing to the study desk; and though, on seeing dozens of flies caught inside the screen, he had a flicker of a headache, it could not destroy his pleasure.

An hour later, having unpacked, stored provisions, and

changed, they carried the wicker chairs and a bottle of Jas d'Esclans onto the terrace, where they watched the light fade from
the hills. Fat bluebottles swarmed around their wet hair. Fire-
flies floated over clumps of borage in the gravel. The white
moon was enormous. They were quiet. Paul felt the sweetness
rise in him like milk, all tension spent, as the sounds and cool
smells of the evening came up around them.

"I remember when I first began thinking about this year. I
wanted a change of skin. I thought of Bali. Then, after Flaubert,
I wanted to go to Egypt, wear a burnoose, aim for something
musky and dangerous, get lost in a maze."

Michael nodded gravely.

"What I'm choosing could be as dangerous—maybe the
most dangerous thing of all: solitude. I know it's only France,
with all mod cons, but these hills are in Gaul, in pagan country.
Varda called these hills heretical."

"Solitude, yes—that might be the last underexplored
country, the last adventure, or it might also have been col-
onized by Cosmo Tours." Michael tasted his wine. "So, make
sure it's solitude and not loneliness—and longing."

"I'm good at feeling abandoned." It's when your jaws
gape open, to take in more air than there is, because you're
suffocating on your own dead air, and the whole thing seems
so final that every other feeling dies with it. It's the sense that
you will die unless someone comes to rescue you. He said, "I
know I'm lonely when at every street corner, seeing an
acceptable-looking woman, I scream inside me, I marry you!
On the spot, now!"

"What a waste," said Michael. "Approach it right: it's
bound to be a feast."

"The whole point about being lonely is that you're at the
feast but can't eat."

"The solitary devours himself."

Paul shrugged.

"Don't worry, Jane and I are never more than a phone call
away if you're starving—but can't eat."

On Jas d'Esclans, their mood got jubilant, and they remembered the golden punkers. "Well," said Michael, "I suppose I ought to be ulcerated with guilt, but I simply can't feel a

thing. The whole night was like a dream. A moon like a morgue lamp and the wind in the empty skeletons."

"Light years from Pimlico."

"Different, so different, that what happened is simply indifferent with respect to it. To Pimlico. Are you following me?"

"Of course. 'Indifferent' is exactly right. A scene so different asks for aesthetic, not moral judgment. It was exceptional, inevitable, haunting, and therefore pure, blameless."

"It could sound convenient to get rid of guilt by saying the thing happened in a dream. But it's true. The Var is prehistorical."

"Till we lay eyes on the 'rationals.' "

Michael looked puzzled.

"That's what she calls the expatriates."

"So it is. Do you feel like going into town?"

"What, now?"

"We could go. Seillans is only fifteen k's. down the road. We could find a café and have a marc."

"No," said Paul. "I'm staying here." Then, on catching Michael's look, he added, "We could go tomorrow. We could hike around the hills." He got up. They went into the living room. The light from the lamps climbed up the stony walls into the high shadows. "To Margot's magic circle," he said, raising high his blood-rimmed glass.

Chapter Three

Paul wanted to be alone, and so he'd been quiet and unresponsive to Michael. When at last the sputter of the car faded and was gone, he began to feel himself expand. He stood on the terrace, looking out at the light above the hills. It rose up in him—ecstasy.

He sat down on the grass and pulled off his clothes, lying spread-eagled under the sun and shaking his head, open-mouthed, gasping, at the extraordinary thing that was happening. The images from the weeks before his flight, once prosaic, were freeing themselves, explosively sweet. They came with an aura that promised others awaiting their turn to explode. Out of their hiding places they came—the yield of weeks of disciplined activity: there had been so much to be done before he could leave. He thought now, the brain is an organ designed for pleasure. Image after image rose up with a margin of luster and power, the nimbus of perfect concentration. That sweetness was pouring into him. It was right that it should be his. He'd done his tasks, striven in the last days to be absolutely good and efficient. At the airport a Gita salesman mistook him for a gym teacher.

He took a chance and turned away from the stream of given images to what he could deliberately imagine. It began with the yacht basin at Cannes or a city like Cannes: with masts, rolled-up ladders, snake-tongued pennants, hulls painted glossy white with raised gold letters, gulls, barrels, ropes—he saw and felt them with a piercing keenness of presence. I can experience whatever I imagine. Overhead, the sun poured down from a purple sky. He was in bliss. And then—from the outside it came in: the yowling, hysterical whine of the power-saw, accompanied by the magnified shrill yipping of a chained cur. He sat up and stared: it was coming from far below the lowest *berge*. How could sound carry with such force from such a distance?

He could taste his mood, like rancid oil; and as if he'd been surprised by a proctor or landlady, he pulled on his clothes, slipped on his espadrilles, and went inside. He smelled the plants—rotting a little in their over-watered pots—and the musty coolness of the stones, then walked out on the terrace again. The din from below had stopped. Then suddenly it started up again and as suddenly stopped for a longer time. He clenched his fists and kicked at stones, hurtling them over the edge.

It didn't come back, the sensation of power, and he knew why: the space in which he could feel happy was narrow and limited. There was a sort of restriction of the space of his heart. It was his bitter secret that irritated every sweetness.

The shame of twelve minutes at the meeting of the American Historical Society—subsection: "Books and the Other Arts." It had begun with a fistfight in the hall with a guard who had tried to prevent him from coming into the room badgeless; Paul had been unwilling to pay an extravagant fee to register for his public humiliation. Wiping the trickle of blood from his nose, he'd walked too quickly into the auditorium, signalling his discomfort at coming late for his own talk. The quiet had settled as he advanced to the microphone. He put his head down to avoid their eyes. They had disliked his success, now they were curious to see how he would try to save face. His hands slipped as he gripped the sides of the lectern. The swift phrases he'd had such fun preparing seemed, as he read, thin and futile, an actual provocation to more harm. It tired him even while speaking—this raging against himself: how could he even have thought he could charm them onto his side? They did not want to be on his side—that was the point: they wanted their superiority. All but one, a woman in her forties, with reddish-gold hair and a beautiful, lined face: she calmly watched him, then got up and left, and he was sure it was not out of contempt but out of decency. No one else left. There was a scattering of applause.

All right, in the end friends said he had outmanoeuvered them with his impertinence. And later, as he'd drunk a beer alone under the awning of an international inside/outside bar, he swore that his sabbatical would clear things up and put an impassable distance between their view of him and his own. It would give him back the honey of experience.

Instead the harm remained.

He was more sorrowful than angry. On this empty hill, his shame and rage would grow bigger. He could no longer think, not even in the silence, which was only a thin curtain concealing the noise of the machinery and the dog below, ready to burst out. He must do something.

He would hitchhike to Seillans: Michael had taken too long to pack and so an excursion had been out of the question; and Margot's 4CV had turned out not to be in running condition after all. Equally, he could rent a bike in the village—but there weren't any really pressing errands: there was still food for at least another two days, and his lighter could do for the gas stove. Anyway, it was ludicrous and cowardly, all wrong, to want to be running away. The trick was to take things a day at a time. The whole of life was only the day; and how, after all, could one fail to use richly and easily one single day? As for today there was, of course, something he could do that would be exactly right. He would write to Margot.

The sun was scorching. In the living room he collected his writing things and stood in the shade of the French doors looking out. Silvery-green gleams came off the *berges*; an inexplicable happiness welled up in him. He walked slowly to the sturdy, weather-beaten table under the chestnut tree and settled.

Writing, savoring his peace, from time to time he stopped to probe with his pen the initials gouged into the wood. There was no MS. There were no traces of Margot here, as indeed there were none anywhere in the house—no forgotten scraps of paper, no medicine bottles, no old boots, no junk mail. She had cleared out. And yet, of course, she stayed—a little in the tapestry, more in the furniture, in the musky air that hung in the dark corners, which he liked to smell: there was a whiff of Margot, certainly—elusive, perfumed, but definite. And just as when he'd been looking for writing paper, he had unthinkingly picked up the folder of her letters and taken them out with him, he now began to read.

May 4

Dear Professor van Pein,

You will want some advice on provisions, so I'll mention the essentials: the local red, the Côte de Maures, is quite good plonk—drinkable and cheap. The best is Jas d'Esclans, which also has a decent white, as does the Coopérative de Fignanières. Otherwise experiment—many of the local farms make their own rosé.

The garden will provide vegetables in abundance, since the growing season goes on till late fall. But that will depend on your willingness to dig your hands into the stony ground. I do, and the reward is great: in the evening, as the light turns purple and gold, I wander through my rows of beans and eggplants and tomatoes and choose.

Herbs are everywhere. They are planted by the wind: you have only to look around. Borage and rosemary are easy to find, but you'll have to go after tarragon with a little more persistence, since there isn't much and it has hardly any smell. The olive trees yield very late in the fall. I left some oil in the house, and there should be small hard olives, too, in various brines. The daily fare of laborers is still a chunk of bread and a handful of olives.

You can buy delicious country bread at Brovès en Seillans—the migrant village: for centuries it perched on the mountains behind you, where the inhabitants lived as shepherds until the Army came. A new Brovès was built in the valley and the reluctant villagers deported. Now the bakery's brick oven occupies a hideous stucco building on the highway where at night delinquents gather.

You can buy good meat in the rue des Minadières in Draguignan or at the market in old Grasse. Both places have fresh pasta, if you eat the stuff. The best cheeses are the *chèvres*, though the locals prefer *gorgonzola à la crème*. It's nice to drive in the countryside, stumble onto a little farm, fight your way through the dogs and chickens and choose your *chèvres* from trays in the cellars. Small farms sell honey, too: I prefer *fleurs de Provence*—the lavender is sickly sweet.

There is one important matter I have forgotten to mention. A day laborer will come to tend the property twice a week. He cuts the grass, prunes the olive trees, waters and weeds, and acts as a general handyman. He has no time left over to help with the vegetable garden. Will you be good enough to supervise him? You may not know a lot about the tasks involved, but a hint of authority on your part will curb his drinking, though you will have to give him a liter of cheap wine before each day's work.

Jules is a man of the Var: he knows everything about growing things. He sniffs out changes in the weather, and his predictions are usually right. He looks like an olive tree himself—gray, gnarled, bent. His language is rough, and he is sometimes hard to understand, but persist: he is a fund of folklore and good hunches. Normally, he comes up with the sun and disappears with it after a long siesta and a chat with you about the day. I am more than a little fascinated by this Jules as he stands, Gauloise pasted on lower lip, wine glass in hand, telling mischievous stories about the mayor's wife and the postmaster, while his golden dog Tintin lies at his feet, drunk on the sun.

Next time more on the rational fauna.

Sincerely, Margot Stevens

P.S. The wine for Jules is the stuff in the workroom—an inky horror that he loves.

P.P.S. I have taken my books with me.

June 10

Dear Professor van Pein,

Thank you for your letter and your readiness to cooperate re. Jules.

Of course, you will need a car. I have something of an old wreck in the garage: it's a Renault 4CV and might not start on the first try. The battery has been disconnected for a long time. But you may use it if you will pay the insurance; it has given me good service for seven years.

I assure you that I have no doubts as to your propriety, and, as my time in July is already promised, I will not be able to meet you. All arrangements for your arrival are being attended to, and friendly expatriates will be only too eager to supply you with a glossary of faux pas.

                                        Regards, Margot Stevens.

Paul was impressed by the seriousness she attached to her concerns, the fact that they were important to her precisely because they were hers, and the rigor of her application to things it had never occurred to him to take seriously. As a result, he again felt disappointed at her having refused the meeting he'd proposed. She seemed unnecessarily peremptory. On the other hand, writing from her house, it could seem that not having met her could be an advantage. Their present relation was bound to be more interesting for having a goal— the intimacy they had not yet known and could not be ruled out.

He turned to the last letter with a familiar pleasure.

                                        July 1

Dear Professor van Pein,

If you could send me the address of your contact in London, I will see to it that a package awaits you with all the information you will need for your arrival.

I promised to tell you about my friends and acquaintances, some of whom you may want to visit when you tire of your solitude. Your closest neighbors live a bit under a kilometer down the road toward Seillans. They are Nicholas Varda and his companion Jean Abels—of mixed nationalities and uncertain age—I believe the mystery is partly contrived, at least by Nicholas. They are loyal friends, function as caretakers for La Casaubade when I'm away, and are helpful and generous. Nicholas remains a wunderkind, full of harmless pretensions and conceits, was, in his day a celebrated theatrical set designer and costumier, and despite his whimsy is rewarding to talk to once he has decided you are interesting. But watch your step with him: he likes administering the truth serum.

Jean is intense and kind, a rare thing—an accomplished writer of children's books and a generous provider: what Nicholas plants and cooks, Jean serves up. If you pass muster—and

Nicholas will put you through your paces the first time around—you will be able to have as much or as little of their company as you please. I have written to them suggesting they call you. Since they have the keys to the house, you will have to have some immediate contact.

Inland a bit, in the next set of hills behind the house, lives a couple who have left Paris to run a farm. They grow olives and grapes and keep a few goats and sheep that they take up into the Haute-Provence in the summer. They are very glamorous. Clara (Beaulieu) is beautiful and about ten years older than Patrice (Grauves), and he is—what?—tall and elegant, with stiff but lovely manners. Their life has the flavor of old romance. They keep pretty much to themselves but will be gracious and welcoming if you show up. I was in the habit of hiking over to their farm every couple of months—their mood is so calm—and sometimes I have even stayed the night after it grew dark before my noticing it.

Generally speaking, social life in the hills can be very busy, particularly among the visitors, who live on the land sloping down to Cannes. It is easy to drop in on them and is actually expected. La Casaubade, however, has been the exception, and people have had to put up with this. I rarely entertained. I believe that privacy is a right that must be fiercely defended.

I imagine that you will be courted in the beginning—a messenger from the lowlands can be a prize to be fought over, so sharpen your wits—to please—and your tongue—to keep your soul intact.

I have notified Madame Onafaro, who will continue to make the beds, air the house, and so forth, at 40 francs/hour.

Best regards, Margot Stevens.

N.B. I forgot to mention that in Seillans, in the old part of town, a composer lives in a fine old house, bare of most furnishings except old musical instruments. He is something of a recluse but erupts now and then into fits of companionability that are worth waiting for. His name is Robert Coustrieu. He is French but has spent a number of years in the States.

Urged on by the confidentiality of this letter, Paul, in New York, had written a couple of pages in which he spoke of wanting to hold still and submit to the cleansing light of the Midi. The letter mailed, he had had a brief qualm about its intimacy.

But now that he was sitting here, in her shade, looking out at the bright liquid light of the hills, those thoughts seemed appropriate; he felt he would be stripped bare and purified. And Margot had picked up his tone, certainly. She had followed up his letter with a postcard: "Sometimes even a lion-heart cannot endure the *démon du Midi*."

He looked up, holding the pages of the letters tightly to prevent the wind from seizing and driving them over the spiky grass.

What sort of woman would Margot Stevens turn out to be? He imagined she looked like the woman at his lecture who had left the room before things had turned against him—only younger. Was she rich? Rich and eccentric? But rich eccentric women didn't often go into the wild to live in seclusion. Probably she supported herself: she could have been a writer—she wrote well enough. La Casaubade itself didn't exclude a taste for sensual pleasure: there were rich woods rubbed satiny smooth and lots of rugs and hides.

On the other hand, the tone of the place was mainly dictated by the plain stone walls and simple windows, evoking the otherworldliness of the Cistercian churches they had seen on the drive through Burgundy, and something more archaic still.

He couldn't know how old she was. She'd lived here for some half-dozen years. She could be close to forty; he strove to think of her as ripe.

Had she lived here without a lover? She hadn't courted company, but had she been able to be here by herself? The hill was isolated—no hand had visibly drawn a line across the landscape beyond the three *berges* in front. Now she was buried in a village in Hampshire found only on the most detailed of maps. Both were places where she could "fiercely defend" her privacy and thrive. Some people prefer to live in quiet country surroundings, but few speak of fiercely defending their right to be left alone; village and country life was usually friendly and sociable. She had not wanted a meeting either in London or in France. You would think she would be curious to meet the man who was to occupy her house, indeed her life, for so long. It had not seemed in her letters that she resented the thought of another's presence here.

What did that mean, that sometimes even a lion-heart could not endure the demon of the Midi? Was she talking about herself? Had she too been forced to leave?

Noiselessly, a golden dog had come up and was crouching beside him, sniffing his bare feet and giving his toes a vigorous lick. Paul ran his hand over the coarse, bright hair. Around the corner of the house came a dark, hunched figure, wearing blue work clothes and an old cloth cap. "*Jour M'sieur,*" he said in a cracked voice, extending a thick, dirty hand. "*Mistral a été bien bon pour vous?*"

"You're Jules?"

"*Ben oui,* and this is Tintin.*"

"He's a beauty." They fell silent. "Well," said Paul, gesturing at the hills, "this is some view."

"Madame always said so."

"How is she—Madame?"

"I don't know. That is something you would know, M'sieur."

"No, I don't. I've never met Madame Stevens."

With a sense of adventure—marrying letter and act—Paul offered Jules a glass of wine, which he did indeed take quickly, and they went out into the shade of the chestnut tree. Jules pointed to a few olive trees that needed pruning; the peach and apricot trees would need extra watering. Paul had trouble following the rasping Provençal twang, while Jules was obviously unused to standard French.

"Does Madame speak good French?" asked Paul.

"Yes," said Jules, "I can understand her."

Paul wondered when Jules had last seen Margot Stevens.

It had been in October, while Jules was working on the olive trees. There had been too much rain, and the harvest was looking bleak. The day of Margot's leaving was unusually cold, and afterward there was a terrible storm. Jules came up early and found her dressed in city clothes. He could tell something was wrong: she was normally asleep when he came, or else she was walking about in an old robe, a coffee cup in her hand, not wanting to talk. Even those last few days, when the young woman had been visiting her, she had never put on anything better in the morning.

Jules figured that someone had died. But when he asked,

she looked at him strangely and smiled. "No, Jules," she said very firmly, "No one has died. You can get that out of your head. Now come in and have some coffee."

In the kitchen Jules could see things had come to a pass. The floor was full of suitcases and boxes roughly tied: she must have been packing the entire night. She said she had to go away, probably for some time, but Jules was to keep working and she would send him money.

"Did she tell you why she was leaving in such a hurry?" asked Paul.

"No, M'sieur. It wasn't for me to ask. But I'll tell you: she couldn't stay put, she kept getting up to look out the door. Then the new taxi driver was there—a bad character, he's not from around here, just wants to make money off the summer people—and I helped carry the boxes out. She shook my hand and wished me luck. I didn't understand, it was all wrong, but women are always changing their minds. I thought she was different though." He shrugged. "Probably gone off after a man. Monsieur Varda says she went to England. She writes him, and then he tells me what to do, and the money arrives every month on time. She should come back though. Leaving this good house!"

"You were surprised to see her go? She didn't usually go off that way?"

"Never. She was always here except once a year at the end of the winter when she went back to America. I know. I've worked for her many years."

Paul poured wine for the old man.

"And you, M'sieur? Are you going to be here alone too?"

"Yes, Jules. I have work to do. I need the peace and quiet."

Jules stared at him for a moment and then got up. "Well, I'll be back tomorrow, to start regular work. I'll be here early, but I'm quiet. Madame didn't like to be awakened in the morning. The mistral will be coming in strong in a couple of days, but it's not bad yet," and off he staggered, the dog leaping along beside him.

The old man's stare had provoked something Paul preferred to forget. The mood of celibacy inspired by Margot's site could prove all too fragile. What could he do? Carol might still be retrieved—sturdy, willing, and bland, her firm, hammerthrower's body a pleasure to watch (climbing out of the bath with dripping thighs) and to hug from behind. But there had never really been any question of her coming. Her preoccupation with her work was total—she traded beans and pork bellies on the New York commodities exchange, a labor for saints of materialism only. How would they prosper here, in a situation calling for continual companionship, which irritated him, but which could be saved only by verbal playfulness, which irritated her? There were too many things she didn't know about him—and shouldn't; too many things he didn't want to know about her—and would have to. Were she here now, there would be regular meals, dinner parties, and new friends called up for picnic outings, no doubt all of it worthwhile, but he had not come to France for good value.

His eyes followed in the glittering haze the irresolute pattern of two red and brown butterflies flitting over the thorny, treacherous mass of brambles below.

Carol was easy, Jen had not been, because he'd loved her. Jen had been his wife. In his last year of graduate school— given a generous allowance by his father, a Wall Street broker who, Paul believed, had more than once sailed a little too close to the winds of the law—he had thrown up his dissertation for a week on the beaches of Martinique. From inside his tent of beach towels, under a blazing sun, he had the rueful pleasure of watching the others jump in and out of the water. Jen, whom he gradually pried loose from her gang, was blond and leggy, with wide green eyes and a mania for speedy movement. Certainly, she was lovely, although he worried about her resemblance to the pie-eyed blondes with inverted navels in the bathing suit magazines he used to scan for relief from his thesis at all-night variety stores on the edge of campus. "Whatever"— as Jen liked to say—Paul made his advances, they were accepted, and after a night of making love gingerly under seagrapes and in the waves, they were in love like pigeons, beak into beak. Two months later, after an exchange of letters, they were married at St. Paul's.

Jen came from a rich family from Cleveland, where she had majored in architecture and literary theory, and Paul wooed her with *Finnegans Wake*. She was unworldly and unread but eager to be initiated, following his lead in a mood of

quick passiveness—he was crazy about her silky hair, milky
skin, smooth thighs, soft cries. She was devoted, he felt mas-
terful, but the proportion soon proved wrong or missing. She
had mainly been raised to be lovely and plan a suburban routine. Walking back home together from the library to their Cam-
bridge apartment, he began to feel suffocated and bored to
numbness, and then the scenes began. His cuts, her sobs, his
analyses, and their bouts of desperate lovemaking sent him
back with relief to the waiting dissertation, and he spent days
and nights in his carrel working as if possessed. Not too curiously, from his quarreling with Jen, he wrote what was judged
an excellent thesis, surprising a number of his teachers who
had considered him not entirely serious. He perceived that
while it was a luxury to have someone to write for, it was
necessary to have someone to write away from. For a while his
sense of his promise and her pride in him carried them along—
she learned to cook well, type his manuscripts professionally,
and indulge the friends he brought home for meals or drinks at
odd hours. He was a promising young scholar with a contract
for a book and a job at a prestigious university: now the American dream could start to come true.

Nothing came true. Everything was dispersion, vexation,
haste. In the intervals he grew cruel to her, teasingly at first; but
his jibes became sharper and sharper, and the more she took,
the harsher they became. "Please don't bolt," he'd say, mask-
ing his panic with weariness when she'd remove herself from
his field of fire. One day she told him she had fallen in love
with a Paraguayan student of chemical engineering. As he felt
her moving away, her eyes once again became mysterious, and
the curve of her thighs promised, and gave, absolute relief. He
persuaded her to renounce Dolfo; and she began studying
acrylics with a born-again Kitchen-Sink Realist, a graduate of a
technical college in the Ardennes. Peace descended, but Paul
could not stop hating her for boring him. Finally, one morning,
while he was holding a seminar on the master-bondsman relation, she packed her bags and flew home to Shaker Heights.

In the months that followed he courted a lanky acquisi-
tions librarian from Ceylon (was it empathic mourning for Jen
that dictated his choice of erotic subject?). Fighting his grief, he
published his dissertation. In the next year or two, as Paul went
on writing on his word processor, sex was no longer a con-

tinually worrying undertow: he put together or was invited to the occasional dinner and small orgy from a network of detached but friendly career women, former graduate students who had failed to find teaching jobs. His men friends had one by one settled into their marriages, but he felt no loss as he dined at hastily assembled tables in cluttered apartments. When a sleepy child crept in during a heated exchange to lean its head on its father's lap, he pondered the prospect but felt no hooks get into him. Although his friends called him "bachelor" with only feigned envy, he would not suffer the question of whether or not on his deathbed he was going to be invaded by bitter thoughts of the ingratitude of his children.

On a transatlantic flight returning from a summer in Vienna he met Nina—English, Polish-born, tall and thin, with short black curly hair and pale skin. She looked like the naked woman who had posed for Grete Buysse's *Fallen Angel*. She was flying to New York to organize an exhibit of eighteenth-century drawings showing everyday life in London—she was "taking a header at Hogarth," she said. She talked with madcap speed about the spatial relations of display while finishing three splits of champagne, until she put her head on his shoulder and fell asleep. She "liked the way his mind worked" and thought him "funny." By the time they had landed at Kennedy, he was breathless, and she said she would come home with him. Euphoric weeks followed, when he winged his lectures brilliantly, he thought. A student reported, "Professor van Pein's lectures are always well-prepared, but maybe he should begin preparing them before he comes to class." Still, this was to praise with faint blame where students (or their attorney brothers) threatened with malpractice suits professors who lingered in lectures over unscheduled books. Paul had little need to write; he could think only of Nina and of replaying his experience of her; it was richer, fuller, and headier than anything he'd known. Without imagining what he might be in for, he wrote her sonnets—by hand—prepared a picnic at the Cloisters and a weekend in Easthampton in a borrowed house, and cooked for her, waited for her, imagined their future together. . . . She half-moved in with him, shoving aside his jockey shorts to make room for hers; charmed his colleagues—the one or two she could stand; read his book and surprised him with her comments; and made love to him any time of the day and night. Sometimes she would call the office and leave a message for him: "Come home ASAP"; and once she sauntered into his narrow, crammed study, locked the door, and took her clothes off to try on an antique garter belt she'd found at a nearby swapshop.

Her work went well, and she made a number of friends. Sometimes she stayed downtown, sometimes Paul went with her; other times, though not often, she just hung around the apartment, reading *Middlemarch* for hours, without a word, without stirring.

On the Monday after the exhibit had closed, Paul came home from a committee meeting to find her sitting in the dusk, drinking a whisky, waiting. "You know, love, it's time I went home."

The words hung there, didn't settle, never would. Despite his arguments, tears, and even—to his eternal shame—suicide threat, she was gone the next day. He phoned her, wrote her, followed her to London, but she could not be retrieved. She was married, it turned out, to a Pole like herself—in his fifties, a writer of stern, comminatory essays on the Americanization of England. They would have no children, and occasionally she would lose herself in a love affair—she liked Paul very much, she said—but she would always return to the large, untidy house in Hampstead.

He watched the burning hills. The years had passed; he began and finished his second—not overlong—book. He was assured of a professional foothold. The amateur gymnast Carol had come along to mollify the pain of Nina's absence. His besotted fits of grief and rage became a memory.

The telephone was ringing. He went into the living room and lifted the receiver.

"You must be wondering why you hadn't heard from me." The voice was plummy.

"Could be," said Paul, "if I knew who you were."

"What am I thinking of? Of course, my dear fellow, I'm Nicholas Varda. Welcome to the Var. I've been remiss, and I've made you unhappy."

"Not at all," said Paul. "Thanks for the keys."

"I must know how you like the house—Margot's little cathedral. A little heavy on the visible stones, eh?"

"No, I like them. They're light and uplifting."

"Those walls will pose you a threat in winter, my dear, which can be answered only by *Sitzfleisch.*" Nicholas chuckled. "I did get that right, didn't I? You're a specialist in German?"

"No, not at all. I can read German though."

"Well, you're obviously very serious. And Margot seems to have a high opinion of you. How is your formidable landlady?"

"I really don't know. I've never met her. I had hoped to when I was in London, but she didn't think it necessary."

"That's Margot. She keeps out of your way until she comes into it. Then you're in her way—until she knocks you out of it."

"Why did she ever leave this place?"

"Why indeed? We were at breakfast with friends from India, and then Margot was at the door. She was leaving, she said, and would we look after things while she was gone. I had hoped we would get on doing our troubadours this winter—her Provençal is quite good—but no, she had to go right away."

"That's odd, I suppose. Why did she have to?"

Nicholas was quiet for a moment and then spoke in an altered voice. "She was probably fed up with the gray. We had a terrific hailstorm later that day. By the way, how's your Provençal?"

"Not too *gai.*"

"Well, I bet you're very clever. You may do. We'll find out, you must come and see us. Would drinks tomorrow suit you? It'll be just us. We like to lie low till the barbarians have left for the brumous North."

"I'd love to," said Paul.

"Good. By the way, have a look at the peaks from the back path. Try it with Cézanne's eye."

"I will."

"But if your mood's more buoyant, go out on the terrace: the sky's Tiepolo."

Paul laughed.

"Or if you're surrealistically inclined—and you sound that way—wander around Seillans: Max Ernst lived and worked there once. About seven o'clock?"

"Fine."

"*À demain.*"

Well, Margot had vouched for this Nicholas Varda, so

there was more here than met the ear. She had said he'd put you through your paces; the first telephone call was presumably part of the rite.

There had been some mystery, then, about Margot's leaving. Had something terrible happened in the house or in England to draw her there?

Paul returned to the chestnut tree, happy he could write a letter that would only strengthen their bond. He'd dwell on his elation at the house and the kindness of Jules and Varda.

When the noise of the chained hound became unbearable, he went back in, opened a bottle of Jas d'Esclans, and continued writing, while taking glimpses of the hills through his study window. Varda might be arch, but he was smart about the view. Cézanne was dead on.

At sunset, everything quieted down. He walked for an hour around the property, confirming Margot's description of the rosy scented evening and the hunt for herbs. He felt exhausted by the howling of the dog. With what pieces he could put together from the day for happiness, he went to bed under the open window and watched the stars until he fell asleep—waking once, abruptly, from a shock of strangeness, before falling back into his pit.

Chapter Four

As Paul walked down the road to Varda's place, he felt the mistral in the brisk dry breeze blowing at the back of his neck. The sky was clear of haze, the air golden, the ground rocky and uneven underfoot. Deep furrows pointed to furious rains the past winter and before. The pale-green, grey-green, gold-silvery-green of the *berges* was broken by dusty lavender bushes, stony trunks of olives, and brambles laden with berries too available to be considered food by the locals. Butterflies darted among clusters of small wildflowers, barely distinguishable from them, winking brilliant lemon and white. The cicadas rose in a din.

He had spent the day in the renovated 4CV, concentrating on rugged roads as he drove from village to village following Margot's clues to food and wine. He had recovered from the dust and tedium by rereading Flaubert's letters from Egypt, happy at the force of his reactions. It had been one of those lucky reads without impediment, when the personality of the author and his own fused in the single crystal of the time between. He'd felt sorry having to put down the book and postpone the urge to start writing, but he would begin the next morning. It was crucial to have a schedule. He had a new book to finish—and if it was hard to write, the result of not writing it would be even harder.

Until last year, writing had been for him the simplest thing

on earth, and he could only wonder that so many, greater than
himself, had been satisfied with a mere page a day. But lately
he had felt his thoughts slipping out of their accustomed
grooves and getting lost on their way to the monitor.

Nowadays, the whole process was so odd, anyway. Once
people had thought their thoughts and written them down
(with pen and ink) as part of the long journey into books—into
artifacts so much more stable than their bodies, their thoughts,
and their selves. But now, given the PC, keystrokes preceded
thoughts—the very strokes that, conveyed by disks to printers,
inked pages. The permanent book was being produced before
the perishable thought. He did not, however, explain his block
with this conundrum.

His subject was modern European cultural history; he saw
connections swiftly and was quick to publish them. This habit
annoyed some of his specialist colleagues, like Dutton, his
Chair, who thought his facts selective and his syntheses prema-
ture. But, Paul maintained, the major correspondences of an
age mattered too much to sink reflection in the quicksand of
archival detail. Works of scholarship were also books to read
and therefore, like movies, had at least to be charming. They
needed rapidity and sweep; they had to be page-turners. He'd
had his greatest success with newspaper reviewers—his second book had got a full page in the *Village Voice*, an event which
infuriated Dutton, who wrote in professional journals read by
an average of 1.7 readers. Paul's essays on the poor house in
genre painting and the commodification of melancholy were
known from SoHo north to Union Square.

There had been one setback. While he was away at Oxford, a theory eraserhead named Bahdaffi had poached on his
domain and smeared his second book, rejoicing the other
oblates who sang together at the Little Church of Deconstruc-
tion around the corner: "I believe, yea, I believe: all is Textual."
Paul faced the great academic question: to ignore the attack
(politically irresponsible) or write a harsh rebuttal (and wear his
pride upon a floppy disk). But over a decanter of port, delivered to their places at high table by a little silver locomotive that
circled round and round, an older colleague dismissed the insult, likening Bahdaffi to a tree snail, which secretes from its
head a carpet of slime to advance on.

With this rite of passage over, Paul had every reason to enjoy his work. He was popular with his students, who turned out in numbers for his lectures. They were mostly underclassmen, curious to watch him associate novels and railroads, pocket matches and cameras, the Taylor speed-up system and the turn-of-the-century brothel. Paul was a bright performer on the stage of college teaching, which his father liked to call the lowest paid branch of the entertainment industry. But his facility in the performing arts could hardly be of much use to him in these hills, before an audience of moles and ravens.

What could his new book be exactly? His grant proposal had been written on the basis of an idea some years old. But Paul had little interest in carrying through his plan to link perspectives of Degas and Klimt with urban street lighting and jagged narrative in Flaubert and Musil. Now all the cross-tying seemed flimsy and meretricious. Everything, it seemed, could be connected—even the act of putting connections into question—which promptly disconnected everything.

He quickened his step and jogged into Varda's driveway. The thick wooden door opened to reveal a slim man with a large smile, cigarette in hand. His graying brown hair was collected in a bun; he wore a green and pink wool shirt and workman's denim trousers, with a variety of straps and buckles. He reached out a sinewy arm. "Paul! I may call you Paul, mayn't I?" His voice was throaty. "Hullo. I'm Jean. How nice to have someone up the road again."

The room was very different from Margot's, although it too had three French doors facing onto a terrace. The walls were cream-colored stucco, every inch covered with paintings, batiks, icons, wooden candelabra—mementos of a thousand trips. There was a deep sofa on which were heaped carpets, blankets, shawls, pillows; and every table surface was covered with stones, reliefs, fans, petrified insects and ferns, books, magazines, and newspapers. Through it all there seemed to reign a single mood: the clutter was actually a collection. "Figure it out," Paul could almost hear Margot whispering confidently in his ear.

Now stamping in from the terrace came a large, top-heavy figure with shaggy gray hair and gleaming blue eyes. He wore jeans and espadrilles and a cotton navy surplus shirt. "Do you know," said Nicholas, pointing a finger at him, "that a thousand years ago the Saracens invaded these hills? Well, it happened again today. I caught a bunch of thugs poaching on my property: they would have ripped out the tomatoes if I hadn't got to them in time. I mean it too, I shall get dogs and guns. I'll protect myself, or perhaps you think that isn't Green enough?"

Paul smiled and shook the proferred left hand. "I don't know. I'm sorry barricades are being raised in paradise. Still, if need be?"

"Need be," said Nicholas.

Jean said, "Come on, Nick. Let's not bombard Paul with it."

Nicholas glared out the terrace door at the garden, shook his head, then went off to get drinks.

Paul and Jean came out onto the terrace and sat on a brightly-striped bench. Jean said smiling: "I don't think there's too much to get upset about. It was unfortunate, an isolated incident. Nick was taken by surprise, though I admit they seemed a nasty bunch." He shrugged. "So tell me, how do you like your house?" There was something easy and companionable about Jean despite his haggard looks.

"It's a fascinating place," said Paul, "and, of course, Margot is a fascinating woman." He was about to start gnawing his bone, but Nicholas was standing there, his presence commanding attention. "You see," said Nicholas, "I'm utterly domesticated." He nodded toward the tray he was carrying, with drinks, olives and something indefinably gray. "Actually, I'm crazy about pottering in the kitchen after a day's work—or warfare. I have some of my most heroic visions as I chop and sauté." He pointed to the platter: "You like little *goujons* deep-fried, don't you?" Paul laughed out loud, and Nicholas looked at him with parodied alarm before continuing: "You've probably realized that most of the expatriates here are food crazy— it's a foraging and food-preserving society. We haven't got to that, though; we don't subsistence farm. We leave that to the ex-executives, who've fled boardrooms for *mas*, to grub away like the peasant forebears they've spent two generations putting behind them. But then we don't exactly get the smart set around here—you'd probably like it better in Cannes, living a life of noisy desperation."

Paul smiled. "I haven't decided anything for certain. So far I like it here a lot."

Nicholas looked pleased.

"If you're not foragers or preservers," continued Paul, "what do you do?"

"I don't know. Jean, what do we do? We live here. You have to remember, first of all, that I've had this house for thirty years, and before that, Jean used to come to Provence as a child. In other words, we were here long before the others. This isn't a cheap retirement."

"Before we came to stay permanently," said Jean, "we used to spend vacations here; this was our secret place. When Nick had finished a play, we'd usually come here for a breathing spell."

"I used to do preliminary designs in that room," said Nick. He pointed backward to a hexagonal mullioned window. "It was during a winter storm that I did my sets for the Ibsen cycle. We still work, you know, but perhaps we are essentially preservers."

"Of what?" said Paul.

Jean intoned, as if he were repeating a lesson: "A certain style."

Nicholas was now doing more than preserving. From notes taken over the years, he was writing a history of set design from its earliest beginnings. He had finished Rome and was pushing into the late Dark Ages. Jean also was writing—a children's book retelling ancient myths, especially their local transformations in Southern Europe. "At the moment," he said, "I'm studying the Albigenses. Their liturgy is pagan, Christian, and Mithraic. For example, they worshipped the pelican who kills and then resuscitates its young, the symbol of a vengeful but loving god. We have an ongoing debate, by the way, about that big tapestry on the north wall at Margot's. Is it of Albigensian inspiration—I mean, much diluted by folk conceptions? What do you think?"

As no one could be sure of the dates involved, Paul promised an opinion at their next meeting and then, at Jean's urging, began to explain the work he did, for Jean recalled having read a review of his first book, *The Logical Image*. He discussed with Nicholas and Jean for a while literalized images and sadomasochistic syntax in Austrian painters and writers at the turn of the century. Then all of a sudden he heard something stilted—more remote, perhaps, than false—rise up in his speech, as if he were on antihistamines, and he began to stammer. "I'd rather not go on," he said, holding up his hands, "because I'd really have to show you some pictures." He paused and began again. "Tell me, you know why I'm here, and I know why you're here. Why was my landlady here?"

"Well you may ask." Nicholas did not sound eager for the question and disappeared into the house to get some more to drink.

"Jean," Paul asked urgently. "How old is Margot?"

Jean thought. "Maybe forty, maybe a bit younger."

"She came here young!"

"Yes, she's an exception, aside from us. We're the only ones who settled here before she did. She's special in a lot of other ways—you should know this before Nick gets started on his theories. She came alone, and no one I know has ever been to stay with her. Everyone around here has a steady stream of visitors, specially during the spring and summer—even we do."

"Why do you say that?" interjected Nicholas as he re-emerged. "Someone did come last summer: Jules sent a young woman up to Margot's house."

"But we never saw her, and when I asked Margot about it, she said I should stop paying attention to every bit of gossip I heard. Margot can be quite ferocious."

"She's intelligent," said Nick, "what else?"

"The big question," said Paul, "is whether she came here to run away from something."

"She's a damned attractive woman. She has those Titian colors, you know—crazy hair and skin like thick cream."

"Are you suggesting she ran away from someone?" asked Paul. He had not run away when Nina left him. If he had run away now, it was not on account of a woman.

"Did I say that?" said Nicholas. "Margot was actually married a couple—or was it three?—times. You know how you Americans are about marriage: you marry on the rebound from the woman you loved too much to marry."

"That's news to me," said Paul.

Nicholas waved his hand. "We had a chuckle about number two: a troubleshooter of some sort—mucky trench coat, minicameras, the whole spy kit. They travelled together. He landed more than once in some god-forsaken jail in Africa, with Margot having to run for consular aid while he sat there on principle."

"He seems to have been a charmer all the same," interjected Jean. "She liked him enormously."

"He ran off with a native activist in Biafra. According to Margot, she was relieved, though of course she must have been furious, too, considering all the trouble she'd gone to."

"She never seemed bitter about it. She's always spoken about him with affection."

"After all, Margot has feelings," said Nicholas.

Jean cackled. "Nick's just quoting me saying that."

Nicholas looked annoyed for a split second, then turned toward Paul in a lordly manner: "My dear fellow, you must stay for dinner."

The three of them went into the large, bright kitchen. Paul half-sat, half-leaned against a high wooden stool while the other two weaved around him in a nice, efficient dance— chopping, slicing, laying out heavy ceramic dishes and cups. Nicholas, who wore a striped apron on which he kept vigorously wiping his hands, started again on the intruders, speculating about their having come west, probably, like Dionysus from the Indus and complaining about the ineptitude of the local gendarmerie.

"Were they East Germans?" asked Jean, who had not seen them.

"More mixed, but certainly Huns: ugly, unkempt, uncouth. You mark my words." He shook a knife in Paul's direction. "They are omens of what's coming, the scum off the cooking pot—overdrugged and underdisciplined."

"What harm did they actually do?" said Paul.

"They were trespassing, that's what. They knew perfectly well just tramping on over here was a provocation, an act of war. I could see it in their faces as I shouted at them."

"If thugs come here, how could Margot feel that she could leave her house empty until I came? Perhaps she didn't know she was going to be gone for so long when she left."

"That's true," said Jean. "You're right. She's up to something important, or otherwise she'd be here."

"You mean you really don't know why she left?"

"How should he?" said Nicholas.

"Jules says a man's involved."

"What else would he say?" Nicholas shrugged. "At least she's true to form: *Margot*, from the Provençal, 'contriver of mysteries.' "

"That's Nick's little joke," said Jean.

"By the way, how do you like her letters?" Paul asked. He sat with his face averted from his hosts, anticipating their resistance. But he glimpsed Jean smiling, so he went on. "They're really quite good, but I don't get as much out of them as I'd like. Of course, they're mostly informative. But I think some of the plainness is a mask."

"Well," said Nicholas, "I can't think she made all the letters she sent you masks—did you say that? What's the mystery? She's not having a personal relationship with you. First of all, she wanted the house to sound interesting because she needed a tenant. Then she wanted it to sound interesting because she wanted you."

Paul heard this plain truth differently and felt a thrill. He spoke rapidly, "So her first letters would be the least revealing. But the moment I became her tenant, her intentions would have changed. We've been writing letters ever since, and I take it that you have too."

"What about the house?" said Jean. He motioned them to the table. "The house can't hide its intentions. And they're hers."

Nicholas demurred. "Even if her house isn't a showcase— and heaven knows few enough people ever saw it—there's still the matter of what she wanted to project. Most civilized people have a fairly clear idea about what they want to seem, and houses get put together accordingly. So there's a bit of display going on there too in the very absence of display. In Margot's case, there's the initial, stunning impression, and then of course one starts to wonder about what's not there. No personal mementos, no things acquired on trips, no pictures, no photographs. That, I think is the crux: she's an impersonal woman. It's something you don't realize right off because she has the knack of creating an air of conspiracy. You share confidences, but in the long run, when you try to piece together what she's given, you discover that it's only you who've revealed anything that matters. We've both had this experience with her—as we realized, especially after she left, and we tried to figure out why. The stories she told us were never really about her—like the epic of her second husband—though at the time she told them we were practically reeling from the privilege of her intimacy."

Nicholas and Jean continued to look absorbed and animated by the conversation. This pleased Paul: it meant that he hadn't seemed obsessive. On the other hand, his very success was making him uneasy. If he had succeeded in involving them in his concern with Margot, he had alienated its intensely private mood. For every bit of information or speculation he got, he had to reveal the part of him concerned with her. Worse, it amounted to a betrayal of Margot; it was mean-spirited, not because he wanted to know more about her—he had the absolute right to know as much as he could about her—only, the pursuit of that knowledge had to be a private matter, not something for the three of them to slice up with chard tarts and wash down with plonk in a cozy farmhouse kitchen. Still, Paul was well aware that it was he who had started the conversation. With Margot he had painted the circle of their complicity that now warmed itself in the glow of an old copper lamp.

Paul said, "Sometimes we say that a house makes a statement, but in most cases, that statement is unreadable. I disagree with Nicholas: I think that few people have a distinct notion of what they want to seem, and just as most are careless with their words, most do not know how to say with their things what they are. You, Nicholas, I'd say are reasonably fluent in that language!"

"Yes," said Nicholas, "I speaka da things."

Jean laughed, and Nicholas began a, for him, serious harangue on the dangers of separating form from function. Houses should be built to reflect the meaning of life—which professors and other clergy identified with higher pursuits. They were wrong: the meaning of life was the happy exercise of lungs, guts, balls and such things; and builders of houses should remember that.

"That may be," said Jean, "but I think that the main statement of this house is a confusion of tongues."

"No. Organic eclecticism, a museum without labels."

By the end of the evening, their rapport was still holding
firm. Paul heard them promise other evenings and outings, and
he stepped out into the dark with a borrowed flashlight and
headed up the hill.

As the cool night air—the mistral alive in the biting tang—
cleared the haze of talk and wine, he concentrated on Margot.
She would be not only a companion of his voyage; she would
be something of a guide—even a goal. Not literally, of course.
It was not as if this entire outlay and risk had no higher purpose than uniting them. But as the taste of the desert pear is
neither in the fruit nor in the palate but in the collision of the
two, his goal would be not Margot but the meaning of her effect
on him, rightly considered. Stumbling over the stones and ruts,
looking up to marvel at the clarity of the stars, which in Cam-
bridge and New York hardly existed, and taking in the night,
which he normally felt as only a vague oppression, he strove to
fit into a rough picture the pieces of her he'd acquired. There
were certain obstacles.

For example, her three husbands, about numbers one and
three of whom he knew nothing. If she loved men so much, it
was unlikely that in her thirties she would undergo so radical a
conversion to austerity as the bare walls of her donjon implied.
And if she had left suddenly on account of a man, then the
austerity thesis was false. It was furthermore unclear whether
Varda knew more than he was letting on. Sometimes he
seemed to say that she'd left for no good reason, other times
that the reason must be a good one: otherwise, she would not
have left the house to rot.

How much knowledge of Margot was contained in even
the most coherent of pictures? Could it tell him what she'd
thought and felt when she was walking to La Casaubade after
supper at Varda's? Did she take from the crisp air the same
release, and did she too disparage personal talk as careless or
deceitful, a sop to be tossed to more interesting purposes?

At the house, turning on lights and seeing the stone walls
and the tapestry leap alive, he was overwhelmed by something
absent. He was its mask, and it could smash him. He walked

cautiously between kitchen and living room, touching the objects in his path—table edge, gardening journal, stone wall—as if to measure his strength by his mastery of each in turn. Of course, there was always safety in bed; but no sooner had he flung himself down, he grew curious about what he still might find below and came downstairs to pace.

He had left the shelter of academic life—the modern monastery for jumbled wills—to find himself adrift in another's world. In the past, in moments of hesitation, he could always correct the drift: there would be papers to grade, quotations to abstract from books, theses to read, classes to prepare; and sooner or later he would be invited to a party, a movie, a meal.

But now, and indeed ever since last December, it was as if he had no world of his own—if "world" meant requirements that engaged you. On the surface he functioned: he had been himself this evening; on the trip down to the Var, he and Michael had got on well together. But a feeling of recklessness was growing. It must have been gestating a long time, long before the fiasco, and now it was gathering force. It had urged him here, and it was urging him toward Margot. He had come not only to forget the scandal of the previous year. He would stay, perhaps, to intensify it.

Suddenly he registered as an almost bodily presence his mournful awareness of her absence. That consciousness seemed something wanted by her—as if a sufficiently manifested degree of his desire for her would bring her to La Casaubade.

This was new, this was not the same as before. He had wanted to decipher her traces, but he had never thought of having her there. He imagined the scene—Margot in the great room, sitting on the couch, looking into his face as he brought his face up to hers. He felt questioned to the limit—and excited. Was this what she had meant about the lion-heart?

He carelessly swallowed a marc; and as he coughed, hearing the rasping sound echo in the empty house, he felt his own body as an intruder from some utterly remote and disliked country. The telephone rang. He took a step toward the sound but made no further move to answer it. The buzz repeated itself stupidly in the empty rooms. First he was afraid it would be Margot; then he was furious that it might be someone else.

Chapter Five

Paul now had a routine. Late in the morning he composed sentences on his Compaq portable. Afternoons, he jogged the seven kilometers up and down the hill at a 7 1/2 minute mile pace. At nightfall he cooked and froze food—having soaked fava beans the previous midnight and sweated eggplants at dawn—from time to time scooting up to Bargemon for well water. Outside on the gravel, he would stroke Jules's cat Titi, poke the plump toads that came down from the peak, and rehearse the letter he would write to Margot. Then, at his desk, through the night, to the dum-dum of moths bursting against the screen, he'd write and read against a background of taped Satie and Schönberg, keeping his eyes open for the odd fat fly to feed to the spider Bruno.

There were special occasions—outings to Draguignan, when he might have his hair cut, boots stretched, and the tail-light of the 4CV replaced; withdraw money from the Bank of the Var; buy aerograms, espadrilles, and a 150-watt krypton bulb; visit the pastry maker for a *tarte tatin* and the baker who baked old-fashioned rye bread over a wood-chip fire; pick up some Melitta filters and green cellophane at the cut-rate dry goods shop and *Le Monde* and the *Herald-Tribune* from the stationer's—also draftsman's pencils and a spiral diary with blue squares—then from the butcher, some shoulder of beef; from the grocer's, celery root and duck beans; and finally, from

the bookshop Lo Pais, a Provençal grammar and a volume from
Paris debating the value of the French Revolution. Arriving at
La Casaubade, he'd decelerate by eating the pastry; jog his
route in less than record time; cook a massive étouffade of beef,
flageolets, and chickpeas; and over coffee and chocolate read
his new book with perfect immersion.

His sense of strangeness about the place dwindled as he
kept to his routine. Then, for at least several hours into the next
day, he could count on being undisturbed.

There had been excursions with Nicholas and Jean—the
best to the Gorges du Verdon, where he had seen eagles. They
had also visited the village Fox Amphoux, famous among foragers for its dark and crusty bread. On the main street they ran
into friends—the Wainwrights—who invited them to dinner.
In the spherical, glass-walled living room lined with unread
books, Paul heard them talk about the clarity of the French
spirit, the impossibility of a United Europe where no two plug
fixtures were the same, and, of course, the barbarism of daily
life in America—conversation he found feckless but amusing,
while admiring their enthusiasm for Provence and their knowledge of gardening. They grew an amazing variety of plants and
vegetables.

Before dinner, they urged him to settle, like a large rabbit,
between the rows of corn salad, snowpeas, and New Zealand
spinach and nibble what he wanted. It had all finally inspired
in him such a passion for greens that, once home, he had
borrowed from Nicholas and Jean an old volume of *The Provençal Gardener* and the next day set about it himself.

Instead of writing, he now spent part of each morning
squatting in the dirt and thinning seedlings, cosseting each
small spire with progenitive pride. As he inspected the
grounds, he found raspberry brakes to poach at the cost of
mortifying the inside of his arms, and watercress to collect into
bundles from odd corners of the stream. He stalked wild savory
and volunteer asparagus and felt his arms and legs grow sinewy and the space between his consciousness and his body
contract to an impalpable membrane.

His malaise slipped away—more truly, off to one side. It
became his familiar, but one he rejected like some inconsequen-
tial person as he lived for his new projects. Sometimes, late at

night, in bed, when everything was quiet with the whiteness of a cocoon, his sense of dislocation would produce another form of himself that seemed to float at a forty-five degree angle above his body like a dying soul in a medieval painting. But he chose to keep calm and ignore this apparition, opposed to any sort of emotional traffic with himself, thinking that to keep quiet was the way to help gestate a sense of conviction in his scholarly work. So, most afternoons, if the wind was not blowing, he would return to the table under the chestnut tree to note Frédéric Moreau clutch his fake desires even during the Paris uprisings of 1848—stirring, from time to time, to pull up thistles from the shiny gravel.

He had not wandered far abroad, being bent on the details of field life at La Casaubade. Only in the fall, after the tourists had definitively disappeared, would he explore the region systematically and visit, for example, Camus' grave near Villeblevin, not to mention the summer residence of Mme. Montfaucon, an outing which Jean had urgently recommended. He also ignored the long, anxious speculations occupying Varda and the Wainwrights about the trivial harassments of the band of derelicts, whose first attack, Nicholas swore, Paul had brought along with him on the day of his first visit. On the whole, Paul thought these discussions exorbitant, the passing fears of people whose lives lacked secrecy or wonder. As a result of his withdrawal, his integration into the community remained in suspense.

One morning, after reading most of the night, he dreamt he heard Jules leading a troop of sheep over the gravel. He could not get back to sleep for hours. When he finally awoke, though the day was exquisite deep purple, he was unwilling to get up, having held a lover's conversation with a woman who in the dream was Margot Stevens. It must have been provoked by his sad reflections, before sleeping, on not having had a letter from her for weeks. His dream was his way of calling her up, and she came: Grace Kellyish, as she looked in the early 1980s, though younger—her hair bound back in a reddish-golden coil and her body tall and voluptuous. How happy he was to perceive she wasn't old—was years younger than he could have expected, yet it was certainly she. At any rate, he could not connect her with anyone else he knew.

She spoke with a New England accent—large good teeth, dimples, cleft chin, violet eyes, round rimless glasses. And their communication was so fluent, a feeling probably produced from Paul's belief, when awake, that the style he had invented in writing to Margot was perfectly suited to him.

All day he carried about the consciousness of being in love at a second remove, a mild ecstasy suggesting a fullness of erotic feeling that to be aroused needed only the loving woman. Carnal desire, he reasoned, was the material sediment of this craving, whose better image was the fire of sunset on the purple hills. Next day he heard from her.

August 28

Dear Paul,

I have decided to call you Paul now that you are living in La Casaubade—I hope you like that. Your first letters were a joy to read, and I see that you are now beginning to have a sense of what I feel about my house. The scene unfolds before me in exact detail, almost to the smells. When the wind is down, I too write under the chestnut tree—and sometimes, when Jules is not around, I stay in an old robe for hours, sipping coffee gone cold, smoking a cigarette, and letting the buzz of the cicadas and the fragrance of the thyme carry me into a kind of aery remoteness, while my pen hangs over the page. These are moments I remember best, moments of arrested consciousness. In the late afternoon I, too, often reconnoiter the property, with an eye out for the herbs I'll need for dinner—wild parsley, savory, tarragon—well-hidden and intense, and sometimes if I'm lucky, dark, ice-cold watercress in the crevices of the stream.

Have you planted tomatoes? I miss the spiciness of La Casaubade's. If you put in some now, you could have a crop for Thanksgiving. You must be elbow-deep in blackberries—they flourish particularly where there have been fires, you know. Here they rampage on the slopes at the sides of railway lines— grimy and gray and altogether heartening.

By now you must have met Nicholas and Jean and admired their museum. Try to arrange to be there on your own some time: it can be instructive prowling among their things. I imagine you have mixed feelings—mine are always tinged with irritation toward Nicholas and exasperation with Jean for letting himself be governed. (I admit, he seems content enough, but some forms of contentment are against the law). At least they don't try to know everything about you, like the famished Wainwrights, though their hunger for improvement is of course innocent, even inspiring. In a way the Wainwrights deserve credit: they really care for others who differ from themselves in marked ways—rather unusual nowadays, with everyone eager only to find reflections of themselves in others who have suffered more than they for the same good cause.

In your visits to Seillans, have you run into Robert Coustrieu? The piece I like best is a G-minor piano concerto.

I'm sorry to have been so tardy in replying, but I've been away and have only just got your letters, a most welcome gift.

Yours, Margot.

Paul let the letter fall—he was sitting on the doorstep outside the kitchen—then reread it. He took the intimacy of her tone as her gift. He liked the conspiratorial feel to her comments about her friends. Margot in her robe—remote, her eyes turned to the whitening horizon—was provocative . . . and challenging. It drove away the rather more domestic picture of her he'd had from his dream.

He got up and paced the terrace, pulling up borage from the gravel. The letter said masses but not quite audibly. The dearth of information about her present was frustrating: she had been away, but where? The letter was full of a precise concern for the details of how one lived one's life, or at least how a life was lived where she'd lived hers. She cared about him. But it was irksome that she did not yet think him ready to receive anything of her present. This was Margot fiercely defending her privacy. Her tutelary plant was the bramble. Had she too been scorched and ravaged? Why was the letter also so seductive? She obviously missed her house and her world, so why was she not here?

He spent an hour jotting notes for a reply while composing duty letters he could no longer delay. Then he knew he must escape the light oppression that Margot had produced in him all day—too elusive to be nourishing, too alluring to dismiss. He would go into Seillans, stroll around, and have dinner: there was more than one good restaurant there. He sped down the hill in Margot's car.

On the outskirts of the old town, he walked quickly past the tourists and the raucous, strutting Corsican-looking youths. The setting sun was casting an amber shadow on the old stones of the fountain-rich, chestnut-shaded squares. He went up twisting, climbing alleyways, the stones everywhere the same—small, dark blond, irregular. The town had been settled from earliest medieval times; in the ninth and tenth centuries it had been the object of attacks by the Saracens. The sheen and density of the stone suggested its stubborn withdrawal and sturdy resilience. Like the other hill towns of the region, it still turned a sheer face to the traveler, resisting even the invaders and pillagers of the late second millenium, who had settled at its gates with gas stations, supermarkets, video rock shops, pinball parlors, and clotheslines of plastic flags.

It was moonlit now. A roguish girl in a blue slip smiled down from the balcony over La Chirade. Paul walked on, through an ancient cobbled alleyway, under plane trees, past filmy street lamps. As he began to climb a few shallow, worn, and shiny steps, he heard piano playing. The piece was un-familiar. Though fully-formed, and violent in a way, it had a tentative quality, as if the player were playing it for the first time. Paul lingered—and felt himself pulled into a revery by something nomadic and barbarous in the cadences, as it trans-lated his mood from nebulousness to burning skies and to a place where, sheltering under date palms at a cool oasis, he felt quick hands slip dark, sweet fruit into his mouth.

The backfire of a truck broke off his longing for something utterly dangerous. He imagined that this was the house of Margot's friend the composer. It made him feel provably in-volved in their life together. She had asked about Coustrieu differently, less ironically, than about the others. When one was grateful for the music someone composed, was one also in-debted to the composer? Coustrieu seemed different from her other acquaintances. All the more reason not to knock on his door: she had said that Robert would dislike a visitor, especially an unknown one.

He climbed up to a hotel restaurant he had seen earlier, where meals were served outdoors. A fountain splashed on a terrace overlooking the lit town, the dark hills, and the stars. He went into a familiar world and settled beside the garden, where the air was cool and sweet, ordering a white Bandol which he sipped while glancing at the diners.

There were only a few. A middle-aged couple with a teen-age daughter sat in calm but too accustomed silence. In the corner, a young woman, pale and lovely, sat with a man much older; he was articulate but also circumspect, as if pleading a doubtful case.

At the table adjacent to Paul's were a man and two women in their early thirties. They were speaking English—one of the women with a French accent. The man and the other woman, with a head of red curls, seemed to be attached, but what was their connection with the Frenchwoman? Her black hair was combed back and loose: she was tanned and wore an ivory silk shirt, pushed up at the sleeves and open to a deep V in front. She leant forward, listening to the red-haired woman speak of the good it would do Provence to import the work ethic of the Protestant countries. The man sat between them, leaning back but listening closely. He, like the Frenchwoman, was tanned: had they then spent the summer together? As the hors d'oeuvres were brought, the man ordered a bottle of Jas d'Es-clans. The dark woman eagerly bit into a chunk of pâté while continuing to speak. Her friend touched her arm and said: "*Toi et la bouffe*, Catherine." He laughed. She made a face at him and continued chewing. "I like the way you eat," he said.

"I forgot to tell you; there was a break-in at the café this morning. Plain vandalism: the cash register thrown down and broken but no money taken, posters torn off the walls, curtains ripped, newspapers flung all over the place. The owner's moth-er was knocked over and had to be taken to Grasse. Everything smashed for no reason at all."

"The wells poisoned," said the man, "the spirit of hospi-tality abused."

"Yes, but why?"

"Because they're 'bourgeois.' Bourgeois values deny real-ity, which is pure violence, so they deserve to be smashed."

"But why pick on this little village?" the American woman asked. "It's so remote—hardly a stronghold of bourgeois val-ues."

"It's not really remote," said the man. "It's close to the heart of the affluent. It's that kind of remote place where you go

for three weeks every summer to buy simplicity and gratitude."
He turned to the dark woman: "Do they know who did it?"
"A band of thugs was all they said."

"Oh, imagine what that poor old woman must have felt
when she opened the door," said the redhead. "Were they
foreigners?"

"I'm sure everyone thinks so," the dark woman said. "The
French can put up with deviant behavior, up to a point, but not
property damage; then it's *cherchez les autres*." She spoke with
the enthusiasm of someone who is expected to be witty, and
Paul could not stop turning to look at her: her face lit up as she
spoke. "It's not the first time something like this has happened
this summer, but it's the first time it's reached the village and
someone's been hurt." Paul watched small parallel furrows
form between her nose and brow as she rounded her lips. "The
village is on the alert. Everyone is saying this couldn't have
happened in the old days. They want to believe the old spirit is
still alive and this is only an aberration." The inside of her neck
arched as she raised her head in a movement of defiance: her
neck was tender and long—part tawny, part shadowed. Her
breasts swung forward under the loose silk of her blouse; as
she leaned back, her nipples bulged from pools of shadow
inside the silk. "Behind their outrage," she said, "there is a
certain stoicism I admire—something we decadent city people
have lost." The next moment, before Paul had time to prepare
himself, she leant forward and looked straight at him, meeting
his eyes, and smiled. It was not a provocative or an inviting
smile; it was simply a greeting, nice for its directness. Then, as
though she'd suddenly realized she'd done something awkward, she stopped talking and picked up her knife and fork. A
flush moved up her throat and spread across her cheeks.
Seeing her change, the other two turned toward Paul. It wasn't
quite a concerted front, but their simultaneous show of curiosity made an acknowledgment necessary, in the name of
civility and because his heart was racing.

"I admit," he said pleasantly, "I was listening to your conversation. It's the vice of solitary diners." They looked blankly
but expectantly at him. "There isn't a lot written on the subject
of auditory fetishism; it's still awaiting its analyst. For years I
actually belonged to a club called 'Les Amis d'Auditeurisme,'

in . . . Brussels. We'd describe conversations overheard at the cost of awful lapses of discretion, but the group soon fell apart. And why?"

Paul stared at the red-haired woman, who was smiling at him, amazed. She shook her head.

"Because there's nothing good enough to overhear anymore."

Paul darted a glance at the Frenchwoman. She was barely smiling. He continued: "And you're the exception. Of course, talk in France is always at least animated, since the French like to interrupt one another. In Vienna, say, that's impossible, since you'd miss the verb at the end of the sentence."

At this moment his food arrived, diverting the others' attention. He hadn't heard a lot of laughter though; and while the waiter served and poured the wine, he wondered, head down, why on earth he'd dragged in Vienna and how he was to get back across the Danube. The truth was that he very much wanted to join their world. And while he liked the dark-haired woman particularly, at that moment any other world would do. He loved the fact that their faces and voices were new. He wanted to hear himself saying new things to them; he craved frivolity and invention. Still, the presence of so many strangers at once was making the approach difficult. And now, he realized, he was stuck. So he continued to look down, smiling and pretending self-absorption, spearing his vegetable pâté and feeling hot shame descend along his neck.

"You're American." The banality brought inexpressible relief. The red-haired woman was looking at him with a friendly smile. "We're from New York—the Upper West Side."

"In search of our twenties," added the young man. "We were students together at the University of Avignon."

He looked across to the Frenchwoman. She was leaning back in her chair, sipping her wine, observing him closely. He felt his heart beating. "Yes, I'm American," he said and looked directly at her. "And that leaves you out."

She smiled as though there were already a complicity between them. "I'm Belgian, from Brussels, though like most people I have intensely mixed feelings about the country where I was born. Now I live in Paris. When were you in Brussels?"

"Wait, let's introduce ourselves," interrupted the other

woman. "I'm Ellen and this is Catherine: she's my best friend
in France. And Alan, here, is also my friend."

"A pleasure," said Paul, raising his glass. "I'm Robert." It
sprang out that way. "Are you passing through?"

"Yes and no," said Alan. "We've rented a house from the
mayor for a week. Neither of us has been to the Var before, but
Catherine's an old hand. She found us the house."

"Why don't you have supper with us?" said Ellen, pushing the flowers away and then indicating to the waiter that he'd
join them.

Paul was delighted as he went over to the table. He sig-
naled himself intensely: keep quiet.

They were settled, the three silently cutting their lamb;
they chatted about the restaurant fountain for a moment and
then fell silent again. Now the change felt decidedly awkward,
even though a minute before it had seemed the sweetest thing
on earth, like dancing. Paul was taking unnecessary risks. Of
course he had briefly played before with strangers on a plane or
on a train at being someone else, but he'd never yet tried on a
complete disguise with someone he had truly wished to know.
The mask he was assuming made him feel an outlaw, especially
as he was involving Margot through Robert.

"I'm an old New Yorker too." He smiled at the two Americans. "But I've lived in this part of the world for the last ten
years. I have a house in the hill behind here, but I go back to the
States once or twice a year to see friends. And when the mistral
comes down in winter, I go up to Paris."

Even Paris was thin ice; he would have to keep moving.
He began a giddy account of his life as a writer of popular
novels, keeping his nom de plume secret behind suggestions of
modesty. He implied that they knew his work well enough but
that he was not about to admit to writing tripe. So Robert became a professional novelist, a semirecluse in the hills of the
Var.

"Do you live alone?" asked Ellen.

He nodded.

"I suppose men of your age and accomplishment don't
live alone unless they want to."

"I find putting up with my own company enough of a
struggle."

"You never lived with somebody else?"

"Yes, I did, but that's ancient history. What is called domesticity I found a continual trial. Not that it didn't work, or at any rate take place: I found it a trial to figure out why I should want to live beneath a satin coffin lid."

"Perhaps you don't really know your desires." Now it was Catherine, looking at him with raised eyebrows and much less of a smile than he had expected to find there, though her eyes seemed dark and deep enough to make annihilation attractive.

"You're probably right. But at least I've ended up knowing what I take to be my desires; and getting along with them"—he wished to suggest that his desires were too intricate and refined to be capable of being much or often satisfied—"is already something of an ordeal."

"I guess getting clever like you is what happens when you live alone," said Ellen.

"Who says he's clever?" said Catherine. "Desires come from others, from imitation of what you think others want or secretly get their satisfaction from. And to learn your desires you have to look around you—more, you have to have close relationships with others." She smiled. "So living alone is actually a mediocre way of finding out what you want. In fact it's a foolproof way of not finding out."

Paul nodded at her; he was too distracted to answer well. It wasn't that the subject didn't interest him; it was precisely the degree of his interest that robbed him of the presence of mind to say what he believed about desires and also to decide what Robert would have to say about them. "I can't disagree with what you say," he said, hoping his neutrality would seem assumed. In fact he disliked her view.

"Come on, Robert." Ellen shoved his arm playfully. "You're not getting away with that. Just tell us one of your secret desires."

"Telling means trusting," said Alan. "Remember the man's a novelist: he'd only make something up."

"All right," said Paul, "just one desire—and I promise you it's genuine." He called the waiter over. "A bottle of Château d'Yquem 1983," he said. And when they groaned, Paul said quickly, "Good Lord! That's only to set the stage for the real revelation."

A large bowl of purple grapes appeared—small and hard, the first of the season.

By now his need for Catherine was moving through him like a force distinct from the pleasure he took in the real woman beside him. He imagined her as his wife at the same time that he desired her precisely because she was unknown to him. He liked her compulsion to be intelligent: it suggested that with her he would be in good hands. At the same time he felt ashamed that he could not stop watching her breasts moving beneath her silk blouse.

When they had finished the bottle, Alan stood up. "Let's go for a walk," he said, "and then we can have a nightcap at our house."

"Why not mine?" Paul was pleasantly surprised by the idea of inviting Robert to La Casaubade.

"That sounds interesting," laughed Catherine.

They wandered through the moonlit streets, their sounds amplified by the stones. Catherine put her arm in his, and Paul exulted in the feeling of her skin through the thin silk. Then Ellen, to his surprise, passed her hand through his other arm, and he was at the center of a world full of power and gaiety. He was fearless.

Alan strode up and down stairways, declaiming in a Provençal accent sentences from Shakespeare and Keats and Hart Crane he remembered from college until someone finally shouted from a dark window for the Balkans to shut up. Intimidated, they went in search of their cars. Catherine would drive with Paul. No sooner did he have her to himself than he stopped and put his arms around her: "I love the way you're full of thought." Her response was direct and passionate. They staggered for a moment in the warm park. "Oh, I like you," he whispered, touching her face. "Your skin." He pressed his face in the hollow between her throat and her shoulder and felt her pulse beat.

She gave him a quick hard kiss, then drew back. "Come on, Robert, let's go. I have my reputation, you know."

"For doing what?"

She laughed.

"I'll find out myself," said Paul.

At the house Paul strode about, showing off the rooms

with proprietary confidence, pulling corks, pouring wine, offering figs and walnuts—and stared at Catherine to watch the form of her acknowledgment.

"That tapestry looks familiar," said Alan.

"The tower in the background is the Château de Montségur, a sort of zodiacal temple. It was the spiritual home of an order of thirteenth-century Manicheans called Albigenses or Catharists. The figures in the foreground are some of the faithful."

"The buggers, you mean," said Alan.

"So you know!"

"The Catharists are probably descended from the Bulgarian Bogomiles; hence the name *bougres*."

"The Bogomiles were fabulous," said Ellen. They believed that God had two sons: Jesus and—get this—Satanaël. I love this name."

"Sounds like someone from a Gide novel," said Catherine.

Paul realized he had been preaching to the converted. "My God," he said. "I forgot. You're all graduates of the University of Avignon. The pelican was probably your college mascot."

Ellen laughed.

"I take it you're all Manicheans."

"Isn't that a logical leap?" replied Catherine, slurring her words attractively.

Paul held up his glass. It was brilliant red. "I give you logical leaps."

"I'm not sure I can drink to that," Catherine said.

"Try something simpler," said Alan. "Simpler—and darker."

"All right," Paul said. "To music, movement, and popularity." Manically happy—the last time he had felt this way was the night in the Ardèche—Paul put Joe Cocker on the cassette player and pulled Ellen into a strenuous, senseless dance. The others followed, and the hours vanished in a confusion of sound, bare skin, sweat, wine, and then the sequence again.

After Ellen had fallen asleep at the end of the sofa, Paul and Alan carried her up to the guest room. Alan put an arm around his shoulder; they stood swaying together. "I hope you won't mind all these strange bodies in the morning."

"Course not. Sleep well."

He and Catherine were alone. Arms around each other, they danced to the end of the tape. "Catherine, how happy I am that you appeared among the fountains."

"Which fountains?" she said, and they laughed.

He kissed her neck, holding her body hard against his. "I hope you can stay for a long time."

"Don't worry," Catherine whispered. "You may have the wrong idea about me." And clinging in an exaggerated way, she laughed.

"Just right, so." His lips followed the line of her neck, and his hands moved with slow pleasure down her back and around her waist and over her hips. Then he was pressing her breasts and unbuttoning her blouse, and there was nothing else in the world but this warm, silky, dazzling woman.

The gray dawn lifted and a breeze came pushing through the shutters. Paul's mouth was dry. He looked at the ceiling, which was becoming water-stained. Then he looked at the mole and tiny pockmarks on the temple of the woman next to him, her lips pale and crusted; she seemed hardly alive. He slid quietly out of bed, tiptoed to the bathroom, splashed cold water on his face, and watched the mist drift and swirl over the bushes and trees.

He went downstairs to the livingroom, staring at the open bottles, glasses, strewn pillows, and damp imprints of bodies on all the chairs and sofas; then outside, where he sank into the chair under the chestnut tree, shivering in the cold.

He wanted his mornings for himself. Foreign bodies were in his house, in Margot's house. What were they doing there? They had come home with him because he'd asked them to. How long were they going to stay?

He'd broken the spell of the place by doing something against its nature—her nature. He perceived to what extent Margot had been a guardian and a steadying presence. Now, he'd spoiled things between them; if he had needed an adventure, he could simply have gone to their place instead.

But by bringing Catherine and her friends here and giving her a taste of La Casaubade, he had made a relationship impossible. It was important to be clear about this: he could never see her again. With the curiosity provoked by nostalgia for what's renounced, and also from a taste for punishment, he replayed the exuberant slipperiness of her lovemaking, her flung-about movements and caresses, her openness in front of him. It was a relief to turn lust into anger. He did not need such memories. What had he done? To himself? To his peace? To Margot's confidence? For God's sake, to their pact?

It was important to act. If he saw them, it would be difficult to avoid some hint of a future meeting, not only with Catherine but with the others too. He would have to leave, but the thought of telling them at the breakfast table was too much. With growing alarm, he saw that he had only one recourse, but given everything, it would not be wrong to take it. It was pardonable, necessary, and in the end it would hurt far less. He would leave a note explaining his hasty departure but also not ruling out a future meeting.

He tiptoed back upstairs, where Catherine was buried in the blankets, grabbed his clothes, and slipped down to the kitchen and dressed. He found a sheet of paper and wrote fast:

This is no way to receive guests, I know, but I have to be in Cannes this morning. Please help yourselves to breakfast— there are good things in the fridge and coffee in the cupboard.

At the end he hesitated, reluctant to continue the charade, but the note was actually an antidote to any future charade, so he wrote, "Catherine, please leave your phone number," scrawled P and, remembering himself, added on an extra leg. For a second he stared at the strange cipher at the bottom of the page; then he dashed out to the car, hit the accelerator hard, and spun away before anyone could wake to the telltale sputter.

Chapter Six

When he came up the hill to La Casaubade, the sun had gone down, and it was dark and chilly around him. He had sped to Fox Amphoux, forcing himself to climb out of the car to linger at an old château. But the scenes of the evening before had gone on projecting themselves in holographs, in which words and images of his public confession last December were embedded: he saw expectant faces disliking and deriding him, and he had not been able to shake them off.

He turned the intensity of his grief into questions. Why had he let Margot get such a hold on him? After all, he had never met her, and she had no claim on his private affairs. Aside from the provocative letter of the previous day, she hadn't written for weeks. So, why did his landlady keep reappearing to chide him for his behavior? He hadn't betrayed her, and the house was his. Yet dwelling on his separation from Margot made him feel only worse—for wasn't she really his great promise of protection?

When he turned into the driveway to La Casaubade, he saw the Citroën was gone. He stayed behind the wheel, at rest for the first time that day.

Inside, the remains of the debauch had been cleared: the kitchen shone, and except for a few dishes and glasses out of place, it was as if no one had been there. On the table was a note.

Robert,
Of course you're forgiven. It's we who should have been up sooner. P.S. Your house is spectacular. We had a long breakfast and admired the view (we're having to drag A. away). The three of us thank you.

Love,
Catherine (94-76-96-11).

Peace had been restored to the top of the house: the beds had been made, and things there were what they'd been before he'd left for Seillans. He undressed and showered, letting the hot water engulf him, and returned to the bedroom, where he closed the shutters and fell onto the bed. At the touch of the pillow, the smell of Catherine naked made him cry out. He tore off the bedclothes, pulled out fresh linen from the closet, drew them tight, and crept between the cold sheets, thinking he could never sleep—until he fell asleep.

He awoke to a magnificent dawn—calm, lucid, and full of purpose. His mood lasted for an hour or so until, after coffee, he picked up Catherine's note and read it, mislaid it, found it again, copied out her phone number, and then lost it completely. That was a turning point. For the entire day, and the days following, he lived in gloom and tension.

He stayed close to the house, thinking that perhaps he'd already had too much of a good thing by coming to the Var, then wondering what on earth he could do about it. He reread passages of oddly accented lamentation in Flaubert's *Sentimental Education*; everything grows exhausted, Flaubert said, except our capacity for grief. Paul wrote down his own thoughts on sacred and profane love, although he feared that the base of his lived experience was too narrow for them to be true. Wasn't it precisely Flaubert's point, however, that this limitation wasn't a personal one? It lay instead with human experience in general—or simply with what was called experience: no human being had lived well enough to guarantee the truth of his constructions. The thought was helpful until Paul wondered on what grounds he could claim the right to share Flaubert's view—and then, still more disturbingly, with what right Flaubert had advanced it. He was jarred by the buzz of the telephone, went for it, then stopped and stood rigid instead: it was as if he were holding his breath for fear of detection. But afterwards he rebuked himself for not having picked it up.

Catherine was not, he knew, the important figure; the question of the other's predominance persisted. Should he or should he not tell Margot about the evening, enlist her no doubt magnificent support to explain the violence of his reaction? He was torn this way and that and finally decided not to: having suffered one unwanted intimacy, it could hardly be of benefit to impose it on another.

He strove to settle into the routine he'd followed before meeting Catherine, forcing himself to work harder. He did not write to Margot because he could not mention Catherine and he did not want to write to her about anything else. But he could not break things off entirely and finally decided to make do with a neutral account.

Cold winds, pale sunlight, and temperatures of sixty degrees heralded the coming of fall. He felt blown clear of all illusion. There seemed nothing left to desire. But toward sundown a nameless melancholy shook him.

He was prey to nostalgia. Imagining the last years together with a Jen grown confident and independent, he was filled with despair at the irreparable loss of happiness—of luxury, gaiety, luck, and sensual joy. This poisoned mist came to fill the gap opened in him by the loss of Margot through the carelessness with which he had abused her trust. But another morning he awoke with a sense of decisive change. He had dreamt that he was talking through a plate-glass window to Jen, who sat oblivious—platinum-haired and beautiful—at a coffee shop on Lexington Avenue. "One million dollars," he shouted, offering her the value of the university tenure he'd got in exchange for her. She did not respond, and through it all he felt the purest form of the grief he'd felt when mourning her, lamenting: "I'm wasting my life, my life is dying, is dead."

Then he remembered that what he'd used to say when he was with her was "I'm wasting my life, my life is ashes!" So how should he shout, now that she no longer wanted him, "My life is ashes because you are not with me"? Realizing this he suddenly felt released.

He wanted an action; in Margot's letters he found it. He would hike through the hills to visit Clara Beaulieu and Patrice

Grauves. It was not yet nine o'clock; the morning was unusually warm. He had a walking map, and to make sure it was accurate, he went in search of Jules, whom he found squatting under a fig tree. It would take a couple of hours, Jules said, so he ought to pack some water. Paul put together a rucksack in which he stowed oranges, chocolate, water, a flashlight, and a sweater and set off with a lift of happiness.

As he climbed, the bush became more rugged, more nearly a single tangle of waist-high brambles, through which flashed the gold of gorse and in the distance the silver-gray of screw pines. At the upper orchards he found a sort of haunted forest—an abandoned settlement with lush lavender, mediterranean oaks, and silky grasses. He met no one along the way. The sun blazed and burnt his face; he lost track of time. Later, as heavy clouds lifted up over the horizon and it began to turn windy, he spotted a large stone house—the stones older and rougher than those of La Casaubade—propped above a small vineyard beside an olive grove. Resting for a moment to wipe the sweat and dust from his face, he saw a tall figure followed by a russet dog coming down the narrow path.

"*Puis-je vous aider?*" asked the man, stopping a few paces in front of him and then kneeling down to calm the restive setter.

"Are you by any chance Patrice Grauves?"

He straightend up and looked at Paul curiously. "Yes, are you looking for me?"

Paul felt embarrassed. "I'm Paul van Pein. I live in Margot Stevens' house. She suggested I walk over to see you sometime. I hope I haven't come inconveniently."

The man was silent.

Paul repeated. "I hope you don't mind my appearing so unexpectedly." Until this moment, it had not occurred to him to wonder about his reception.

"No, no, of course not," replied Patrice, extending his hand. "We've only had the phone put in last week. It's very good of you to come, and anyone whom Margot recommends can't be all bad." He smiled pleasantly. "It's a hike, isn't it? You must be thirsty. Let's go up to the house and get something to drink."

As they approached the orchard, Patrice said, "I was

working on the olives: they look sturdy, but in fact they're temperamental and need a lot of attention. I'm actually grateful to you for giving me an excuse to stop." Patrice's speech was tidy and precise, his elegance was disciplined. He would have looked smart in the tennis whites of idle society sixty years ago; now he wore faded, rumpled jeans. Paul wondered if he was being unreflectively tolerated, or had Patrice shown a glimmer of interest in his visit? That was the point of personal charm: the charmer enjoyed emotional protection, you could not see past the dazzle. Patrice had the pleasant, equable manners of one either well brought up or naturally disinterested. Perhaps his calm was the result of a whole succession of pleasant days. Margot had implied that he and Clara Beaulieu lived in a world for themselves and full of happiness.

"It's much more rugged here," said Paul, putting down his rucksack. "The landscape began to change the minute I left La Casaubade. The hills there are rugged too, but they come off the coast, and they've been plundered so often they're now open and without defenses."

"Certainly it's wilder. I've done your walk with Margot: I felt a change in time as I came on back. Here, life follows rules even older than at your place. Clara and I are intruders with our rational gardening. We're foreigners, even though we've been here for a while and live very well. Common nationality or love of the place has nothing to do with it."

"I suppose that could be uncomfortable."

"How could it be any different? We come from Paris, and when we arrived, it wasn't with the expectation of being made comfortable." Patrice laughed casually as he opened the door of the house. "We had only one illusion when we came—that we could be on our own here in a way we couldn't be in the city. That illusion's held up. To that extent we've been accommodated, so we're ahead of the game."

By now they were in the cool, dark stone kitchen. Patrice took brown bottles of porter from a small cupboard and poured them carefully into pewter mugs.

"I'm glad for you," said Paul, leaning comfortably against an old oak dresser. "I hoped for the same kind of result when I took Margot's house."

"You haven't come with your wife or a friend?"

"No, I came to be on my own."

Patrice hitched himself onto the edge of the plain deal table. "Where do you come from? Are you American or English? Pardon me, you speak French beautifully, but I'm immensely partial to the Anglo-Saxon world. So given your slight accent, I'd like to know what it means."

Paul couldn't hold back a smile of recognition at what Margot had called Patrice's very civilized impertinence. "I'm from New York," he said. "I teach history at a university, and this is my sabbatical year. I didn't want to settle into a research library, so I've come to do some writing. But chiefly I've come for solitude and perhaps renewal, particularly the latter."

"Rather ambitious." They both laughed. Patrice led the way to wicker chairs under a shady tree where three kittens were romping in the grass, chasing sunbeams as they shifted through the chestnut trees. "Solitude can so easily turn into a quite brutal loneliness. So then what's renewed is only something very old and perhaps better left alone. How have you fared so far, though I presume you're still at the beginning?"

"Yes, I've been at it—let's see—for three months. I suppose the great, the unpleasant, surprise is the extent to which I've been, in fact, fascinated by others: by those, I mean, I conjure and remember or who conjure me. I wasn't prepared for that. After all, in New York I live alone, but then again, I'm not alone there: I see people—it's a way of driving them out of mind."

"And the renewal?"

"I don't feel much renewed. But what I feel—a sort of fertile confusion, broken clouds—might very well be its prelude. I've been reading Flaubert; I haven't written a lot. Everything takes so long. But the experiment's still on."

"I hope you'll tell me about the result."

There was a sound behind them. "Oh, a stranger," said a husky voice.

"Here's Clara, back from toiling and moiling." Patrice reached up and touched her arm. "This is Paul van Pein, who's staying in Margot's house."

Paul got up and shook her hand. "I hope I'm not intruding."

"Not at all. What a nice surprise. I was just in the mood for a little novelty." She smiled warmly at him, and he felt uplifted. She was tall and strong—a handsome woman with large, deep blue eyes and ash-blond hair pulled back with a ribbon off a round, tanned face. "So you're Paul. We had wind of your coming, and we were very much hoping you'd be hiking up to see us. We so rarely see anyone. Oh, I'm sure you'll do us good. We'll be able to discuss you for days after you've gone." Her words tumbled out from a mouth full of smiles.

"I promise you," said Patrice "that she'll find every possible reason for praising you. What shall I get you to drink, Clara?"

"Just some water for now. And some beer for Paul."

Paul shook his head and made an involuntary gesture of contentment. He liked being where he was: he liked their courtesy and simplicity of surface. Like Patrice, Clara wore nondescript work clothes. She had no makeup on: there were abundant creases around her eyes and her lips when she smiled. It was a face on which happiness had turned an excess of care and labor into beauty. As Patrice walked away, Paul felt that her inner eye followed his figure for a moment before she returned to him.

"We were talking about solitude," Paul said, wanting to enter her world and matter to her.

She too had her theory—distinguishing solitude from loneliness, detachment from exile, and solipsism from the spirit of community which could flourish even in isolation. She spoke clearly and well. And yet Paul found his attention veering off to the expression of delight that kept moving across her face. The pleasure she took in her own talk wasn't self-regarding but the immediate delight a clear soul takes in its own activity, a soul grown clear from the choices it has made for itself. Whoever sat with her could himself settle, without guile or dissimulation, and be confident of her generosity. It was only the mention of Margot's name that interrupted his reverie.

"You did say Margot?"

"Yes, she and Robert Coustrieu are the purest ones: they live their solitude with the greatest conviction. People talk about them the most, but talk touches them the least. Of course you must know Margot a great deal better than I. Are you and she very good friends?" She reached up and, smiling, took a glass of water from Patrice. "What's become of her anyway?"

"Margot and I have never met. She's living in rural England now, and we've exchanged a number of letters, but Margot hasn't said much about her life at present. She writes about the life she used to live here and seems to miss it keenly. I wonder why she ever left."

"We were puzzled too," said Patrice, "after we first heard that she'd gone. We like Margot a lot: she's a woman of pride and independence. You know she's practically revered by the people of the village. She single-handedly rang the church bell the night of the great fire. We didn't see her a lot, of course: she used to come up a couple of times a year and stay for a day or two. But we feel we know her well because when she was here, she would talk endlessly, wouldn't she, Clara?"

"Of course, we would all talk endlessly!" Clara put her long legs up on the extra chair. "She had to talk her heart out, almost as a physical requirement. She and Robert are the same that way: you won't see either of them for months—no one will—and suddenly they're here—Margot or Robert or both together—rather menacingly quiet at first, even quiet for a long time, and then they're like explosions."

"Explosions—of?"

"Oh, arguments, memories, stories, reflections. Robert's the more overwhelming one, especially as he turns morose just before driving off."

"I'm always willing to hear you on that subject," said Patrice, smiling, "but you did tell me to warn you when you start edging into gossip."

Clara grinned. "Mea culpa—once again."

"Oh," said Paul, "I think it's my fault. But what about making an exception this time? I hardly know anything about either of them, but I feel I want to know them very much. I remember that Margot mentioned Robert in a special way, as someone decidedly worth knowing. He's a composer, isn't he?" And with the memory of the music in Seillans there came, in a flash, his strangely affirming nostalgia for the dark green oasis, deep and hidden.

Clara pondered for a moment, then gave Paul a large smile. "Very well—we'll make an exception. Just this once."

Patrice laughed.

"What exactly do you want to know?"

"About Margot's and Robert's solitude."

"What can I tell you? Because of Robert's music," said Clara, "it's much easier to talk about his solitude. It doesn't quite work for him because he's devoted to his music—though only by fits and starts. I mean he isn't willing to cultivate his solitude. He wants a shadowy, silent, maternal woman to do it for him—by protecting and adoring him, to make it fertile."

Patrice seemed taken aback. "That isn't how you usually speak of Margot," he interrupted.

"I was speaking of the other woman."

"The other woman?" Paul murmured.

Clara nodded. "The woman who was involved with Robert last year."

"I see."

"But I don't want to discuss her. I shouldn't have mentioned her."

Paul said, "I've heard that Robert's house is a kind of museum, full of old musical instruments."

"I don't remember ever having been inside," said Patrice.

"I was there once," said Clara, "about this time last year. It was market day in Seillans, and Robert was lying in wait for me, saying there was something he wanted to talk about. When we got to the house, though, he seemed only anxious that I'd come—awkward and mysterious."

"I never heard about that."

"Patrice, of course you did. Finally, he made a speech about the geometry of field asparagus! That was all very well, but I lost patience and asked him directly what he wanted to talk about. He sank back into his gloom. No, he couldn't, he said, it wouldn't help: it had been a mistake to think of involving me."

Patrice was gazing at her with burning eyes. Clara stopped as if she'd woken from a dream. "I say, I am telling a lot of things perhaps I shouldn't." She turned to Paul. "You are discreet? You can be trusted?"

"Yes," said Paul, "I can be trusted."

Clara looked back at Patrice, who barely shrugged.

"Very well. Robert suddenly said to me, 'Do you know

what it feels like to be divided, exactly in two? I want my peace, I want my music, and I want to find something out. And the exact cost of finding out this thing means the end of my music and my peace.' 'You're talking about a woman,' I said. But he only laughed out loud, rather bitterly, and said, 'No, not a woman.'

" 'Then who or what is the object of this obsession that so disturbs your peace?' I asked, and he said, 'A norn.' "

"A what?" said Patrice.

"A norn."

"What's a norn?" Patrice turned to Paul. "You're the professor: what's a norn?"

"I think a fate or weird sister of some sort."

"I did ask Robert," said Clara, "but he said the word didn't matter. Then I must have looked fed up, because he became terribly embarrassed—you know Robert—and he stood up saying he had already kept me much too long."

Patrice looked pained.

Clara said, "I could kick myself for not having looked up what a norn is. . . . But, wait, wasn't that the day of the hailstorm?" She turned to Paul: "We had hailstones the size of apricots." She turned to Patrice. "That's why I never went into detail about seeing Robert."

Patrice got up and kissed her.

Paul was glad of the gesture but jealous too. "So Robert was referring to a woman—but to a heartless one, I suppose. Margot . . . or the other?"

"I'm not sure. It was evidently part of his private code."

"Having to puzzle such things out is the price you pay when you're the first to break the silence of the solitary," said Patrice.

"He does sound self-involved," said Paul.

"Robert was so reckless last year; he acted as if he'd gone mad, speaking in tongues about bushfires and holocausts. But when we saw him some months ago, he seemed quite calm— for him."

"Was it because he had settled on solitude or because he'd extinguished his norn?"

Clara looked at him and laughed. "You're an angel for asking," she said. "I can't really tell you. He was easier, certainly—more his usual self—so maybe that's what everyone's leaving finally did amount to." She veered off. "You know, in one respect, you two are alike. He kept asking all the time where Margot was hiding. Of course we knew nothing until we had her letter from England, saying that you were coming and would we look out for you. If I hadn't run into Jean in town, I wouldn't even have known she was gone. Certainly we did find it strange, on reflection, that she left without a word."

"How did Robert react when he heard she was in England?"

Patrice got up and went into the kitchen.

Clara leant forward, smiling, her hands between her knees. "You are a nosy one," she said. "I think I may like you. How did Robert react? Well, he happened to be in one of his manic states—he'd been drinking. 'England,' he said, and again 'England, now. And she's run off again . . . under the most mysterious circumstances. These mysteries of other peoples' personalities are to be shunned at all costs!' 'But,' I said, 'you value her so much.' For a moment he looked stricken. 'Better that she's gone.' You know—where did Patrice go?—I think Robert has begun to dislike her."

"But they used to be lovers?" Paul brought this out slowly.

Clara grinned. "Oh, let's just say they go way back."

"Ah," said Paul.

"I don't know all the details," said Clara, "and if I did, I wouldn't tell you. I know, why don't you ask Robert?" She laughed. "I'm sure Margot wrote to him about you too. She seems to have written to everyone."

Patrice returned with an armful of kittens. "I've come back to lay down the law," he said, with a trace of real severity. "We will leave other people's lives to other people. I suggest we take Paul for a walk, it's the best part of the day."

Paul got up. "I should be thinking of starting back while it's still light."

"Of course you shouldn't." Clara stood up next to him. "You can't deprive us of your company so soon. I hardly know you well enough to have a good gossip about you after you're gone." She turned. "It would be mean to deprive Patrice of the pleasure of scolding me for my indiscretion."

"Of course you must stay," said Patrice smiling. "We just assumed you would. Have dinner with us and stay the night."

Paul was elated. He hadn't in the least wanted to start back yet. After such friends and such admissions, the emptiness of his walls would kill him. He had stumbled on treasure: he wanted their affection and their news. This smooth, untroubled love of theirs, in isolation: could it have been won without cost? A price had been paid, he was sure of that, and wouldn't he see signs of that price being paid?

Yet walking across the property with them, he was struck by the effortlessness. Clara talked the most and Patrice came in, curbing and qualifying a little, with good-natured irony. They talked about their plantings—herbs and berries and young trees—and the small details of the care they brought to their everyday life. But as they reached the crest and stood looking out—Clara or Patrice always drawing Paul's eye to the curve of a slope, the line of a cypress—Clara remembered how hard it had been to leave the life they'd lived in Paris. She had been an actress, working in the theater, devoted to good causes—to political, social, and artistic improvisations. She had never imagined there could be any other way to live. Patrice, who had held a position of authority in a multinational corporation, had changed all that. Not right away, of course. At first they'd fought, each fiercely defending his or her own territory. But each had then come to like the manner in which the other fought. Finally, Patrice had made her see that the affection they felt required a soil more natural than strife—a real soil, so they'd sought a third term, an element they'd found in the Var.

While she was talking, Patrice put his arm around her. "Clara, love, why, when you speak about the past, do you always sound as if you're preaching, telling the story of an exemplary conversion?"

"Conversion? But it was all so gradual. At first I thought he was only talking about living in the country, but he meant living off the land. Well, I never say never, so I agreed to try for six months. That was the minimum arrangement he'd accept. The first couple of weeks were awful, really awful. We had a short-legged goat that not only wouldn't eat paper and tin cans, it wouldn't even eat choice hay. We finally found out what it liked: fig leaves! Yes. What things to be thinking about! But finally, one morning, I woke up and realized I rather liked seeing my goat foraging and wanted another, and then my eyes started to see more and want more, and soon each of my senses was hungry for its goat."

"In a word, we discovered by trial and error what we could manage," said Patrice, "and on that basis what we could risk."

They had long left the property behind and were now at a point where the hills sloped down into a deep green valley spotted with autumn brown. Here and there was a shabbily tended vineyard or a stone house in ruins. "What do you think about all this?" Clara asked Paul.

"Ah," said Paul, "At such moments I could certainly commit myself to the Var forever."

"I'd beware of that idea," said Patrice, "unless you do it as we do, and that means ultimately only playing at it." With his hands deep in his pockets he stared almost somberly out over the hills. "Clara and I till the land and cure the sheep, but it's because we want to, not because we have to. Certainly we work very hard at times, but it's disappointment not despair we feel when a crop fails or the bellwether comes down with scabies. And if ever we tire of it, we know we have only to get on the train and we can have Saint-Germain again. We're amateurs of difficulty, but the life of the farmer in these parts is still harsh and brutal."

"And yet," said Clara, "there isn't really any going back again, ever, you know that." She spoke quietly. "But, I say let's turn back and have a drink to the setting sun."

"And to our romantic streaks," said Paul. "May they flourish, though I have a rotten suspicion that mine is going to land me in trouble." At this moment he was actually imagining putting his face against Clara's breasts.

"Now, that" said Patrice, patting him on the shoulder, "is the romantic view par excellence."

They wound their way back down to the house, where Patrice excused himself to go off, in order, he said, to feed the greens before nightfall.

"The sheep drink beer. The rocket eats potash. What a

world," said Clara. She urged Paul into an old-fashioned wicker chaise longue beside the fireplace while she attended to dinner.

Left alone, he found himself drugged with sleep: he could not keep his eyes open, and when he awoke a little later, he felt an overpowering sense of abandonment. He reached up to touch his cheek and found, to his alarm, that it was wet. He started up; Clara was coming toward him. As she bent over, he involuntarily reached out his hand.

She took it. "What have we here?" she asked gently. She tightened her hold on his hand. "I heard you cry out."

"I'm sorry. I fell asleep." He sat up. "I don't know what's the matter." He felt utterly separated from their life, and their life was the only one there was. Yet he was conscious, he was here, he had been found. He wished to speak to Clara, but he could think of nothing simple to say to her that would be true to his feelings. And yet he wanted to speak, to show her that he trusted her—this good and beautiful woman who had revealed herself to be no better than she was, who hadn't hidden her sentimentality, her garrulousness, her busy curiosity. Finally, he began. "It's that my life feels as if it had come apart. I'm so cut off—I'm a damned ghost. I've been what I was, but I'm not anything different yet." He wished he had thought of something brisk and clever to say.

"You know, maybe you're being too hard on yourself. You're probably just disoriented. You've lost your familiar world and your work, both at once, and you're on your own. It's just a question of time."

"Yes, that must be it."

"You must be patient. It could be interesting."

"I'd like to believe that. You know, I've been used to writing a lot, but the will to that has gone. How can I give myself to a future without writing? Of course, something damaging did happen before I came here. And now it's as if my memory had stopped working, as if my past had stopped being anything I care about. So I don't write, because I will not keep the past—and I'm an historian!"

"Look, our first few months were one continual crisis. I also left everything I'd ever known behind, and worse, I felt I'd done so permanently. Nothing was recognizable: even Patrice in this new environment wasn't. Heaven knows, right from the start we hadn't ever shared—what do you call them in English?—'frames of reference.'" She laughed and said, "We had no 'frames of reference'—we didn't even have windowframes. They were rotted, the glass fell out of them."

"But you had your quirks in common."

"Quirks?" Clara thought for a moment. "No, we had no visible quirks. Anyway, the great failing is maybe making quirks out of cathedrals."

"I'm sorry?"

"Making cathedrals out of quirks."

"When we should just put our quirks into hencoops."

"That's right," said Clara. "Come with me into the kitchen. You can help me get dinner. Here, you swing some lettuce."

I would hang for you, he thought. He liked lounging in the kitchen with this woman. It was a pleasure that reminded him how long he had done without it. The occasion didn't present itself when supper consisted of waiting in a crowd at a restaurant serving *New* Jersey cuisine, or being shown into Siberia by a maître d' needing a twenty for mob dues, or else warming up jalapeño-laced cat food from a leaky carton. There was unwonted calm in handling recognizable ingredients in rhythm with a friend, their conversation occasional, funny, and kind. And when Patrice stepped in from the dark, Paul found himself glaring at the intruder. Patrice quickly excused himself to wash the dirt off his hands. By the time he returned—even taller than Paul, freshly dressed in a white sweater, wet hair combed sleekly back, his pipe-thin legs interminable in jeans— the two of them had finished their companionable chores and settled in the living room, waiting for the final ping of the timer to announce that the chicken was done.

Their talk at supper ranged all over the map but kept drifting toward one half-buried lode: Margot's secret life. Paul woke up sharply on hearing Clara say: "I think she also lives obsessively; she's haunted by her memories—her constant, unsettling companions. They're the result of her work."

"What is that work?" Paul asked.

Patrice knew more about it and was willing to talk. "Margot is an anthropologist by fits and starts. It was the day, years ago, that Robert also suddenly showed up: she told us about her adventures in the field. She had gone to an island in the New Hebrides. The days were profitable as she went about with her informant, interviewing the chief, and trying to learn the local language. But the nights were terrible. The sun would go down early; there was no light, of course, except from the fires, but that was not enough to read by. What could she do all evening except sit in the dark? She had no one to talk to, and to light an oil lamp meant to be eaten alive by mosquitoes."

"It was," said Clara, "a prolonged case of the five-o'clock-in-the-morning screaming mimies. And this time, my friend," she said, turning to Paul, "I'll have something to tell you about Robert's reaction. Listening to her he became a changed man, full of rapture and anger. All weekend he kept coming back to the nights in New Hebrides, drilling her on it, however much she tried to avoid the topic."

Patrice interrupted. "Margot did not stay on the island. She returned before her leave was out."

"And her work now?" asked Paul.

"I'm not sure. The house kept her busy. She writes a little—travel pieces, restaurant reviews. She makes up puzzles—not crossword—cryptograms, the sort of thing you find in the *London Times*, something we French have never really developed a taste for."

"That I believe," cried Paul. "She'd like the purity of the strict code, in which everything fits without remainder."

Later, in the strange, though unthreatening bedroom, he saw a woman with red-gold hair, huddled against a post, her eyes wide open, straining to keep in view the walls that stood against the darkness.

Chapter Seven

Dear Paul,

Your last letter was hard to fathom. It's wrong of you to excite my curiosity without supplying details—good healing details of things precisely seen and felt. What exactly happened that night in Seillans? And how can such acquaintances have provoked you into "awkward" behavior? I exclude from this charge the marvelous description of your walk. I was with you the whole way. Wouldn't it be perfect if it were really Robert's music you heard and which moved you so? I'm disappointed that your mood was ruined by the summer people. Some of them are of such coarse plastic I think the Industrial Revolution must have been invented in order to produce objects suited for their diversion.

Yes, the hike over the hills to Clara and Patrice's is a trip back in time. I always imagine I am walking with Rousseau or young Goethe, and indeed I become them. My spirits lift, my footsteps lighten, I hear their words. Reading you, I hear them again. Have you noticed that a place can become a book of all the times you've been there before?

Patrice and Clara are special company. It is only with them, I think, that I let myself go. I trust them, I drop my guard and expand in all sorts of unseemly directions. They improve you at the same time they make you more vulnerable. It's not that I

79

actually envy their union—it's rather that they suggest another way of being, different and probably better than adult solitude. They tap a nostalgia buried within us since childhood. Is it the nostalgia for childhood? No, a nostalgia, I think, we already felt as children—the longing for another country. And these two seem to have discovered it. Actually, I find them rather heady and can only take short visits. I go on impulse, glut myself, then stay away, fasting and repenting. But go again soon, make them take notice of you.

You say they spoke to you about Robert. Now that I think of it, perhaps it would be best if you approached Robert through them rather than through me. It's true that at some point he was linked with another woman—I could never cotton to this Catherine—but that's over now. She's not part of his life nor should she ever really have been.

You must meet Coustrieu soon. I can see the two of you becoming good friends: you'll like and respect each other. Don't be startled by his intensity: if you are, he'll distrust you and shut up completely. His extravagant outbursts aren't meant to make an effect: they come after long bouts of work and solitude.

Here the wet, gray fall begins, but behind the clouds my wine-filled days still burn. Dear tenant, your letters are bittersweet, but I would not be without them.

Yours, Margot.

This had become her tone, Paul mused, moral grandeur and cajoling intimacy, an intimacy conjured through grandeur. Her castigation of the "coarse" tourists was excessive, not at all suited to the plain account of them he'd given her. And what of her dismissal of Robert's Catherine, who'd probably had a very hard time of it to judge from all the clues? Margot felt herself to be a breed apart. And supposing she was, what would it cost to be judged one of her kind? Certainly she included him, but she had also turned some of her hauteur against him.

He had no more of his own wine, so he filled a water glass from Jules's bottle and flailed away at the flies, which, with October, had arrived in clouds. Then he got at the rest of his mail. A postcard from Michael urged him to visit London soon. He imagined the idea for a moment, then rejected it: he was not ready to return to the flatlands. At the bottom of the pile was a letter postmarked Paris and addressed with an old typewriter to "Monsieur le Propriétaire."

October 24

Robert,

I have decided that wounded pride should not keep me silent on the incident of our meeting. I find your lack of courtesy appalling. There are other, more courageous ways of ending a relationship than flight and silence. But you evidently inhabit a world in which the "successful" male still assumes as his prerogative the droit du seigneur. Be advised, sir, that your world is crumbling.

Catherine Lavernier

Even her name was typed. Paul did not know whether to exult or be ashamed. He felt hurt by the accusation but surprised at his power. Then he felt protective admiration for the author of such a letter. It took panache and a lively sense of one's worth to tell off one's disappointer so resonantly. He could write her this, but it was unlikely she'd be pleased to hear it from him. There was no return address—though that was something he could probably coax out of Information. But . . . . His eyes turned again to the beginning of the letter, to the name that had jumped to his lips that night in Seillans. The thought hurtled up into him. Was this the same Catherine whom Margot had just dismissed as insignificant? Could it be? As the identity grew more and more imaginable, an excitement rose up, absorbing him completely. He was conscious of too many thoughts dividing Margot from Robert. He must begin preparing for struggles ahead: if his adventure with Catherine had made Margot think less of him, it would also draw him into combat with Robert.

He needed to have his surmise confirmed. How could he discover the truth without sooner or later revealing his own awkward role in it? If he spoke to Clara, he would have to lie about Catherine, and that would put an end to the prestige of their relation. Besides, Clara had been protective of "the other woman"—his Catherine—and would not talk about her. Margot, of course, had shown herself utterly disinclined. Nicholas and Jean could help. He grabbed the telephone.

"Hello, Jean," he said. "How are you two? It's been so long since we've spoken."

"Is this Paul?"

"Yes, yes, I'm sorry, Paul van Pein."

"That's odd, we were just talking about you this morning, wondering what on earth had become of you."

"I've been writing a lot. The books keep arriving."

"Well, what do you say to coming down and telling us all about it? How about tonight? Nick's making some swiss chard quiches; you liked them the last time."

"That's very kind of you.

"Come for dinner. Eight."

"Thank you. I'll see you later."

Paul weeded the terrace with adrenalin-charged efficiency, cleared the back of the garden, and chopped and laid down wood in uniform stacks to prepare for the coming storms. For the first time this year, it seemed to him, he could savor the pleasure of justification. His remoteness from his old concerns was turning into gold, exile into ecstasy. The piles of books, daily arriving—books he'd so carefully assembled in his over-crowded office—seemed heaps of folly and pretence and a de-cidedly meretricious form of them too. What mattered were the combinations that now turned in his mind, sequences thrown up by lived experience and just in time; these alone were real. As he hacked joyously at the logs, he felt that his life was on edge, depending entirely on what was now beginning—and hence on the accuracy of his blows. It was as if he had gambled for years and now stood in an empty space, his breath hardly coming at all, yet confident that he would hear the call sum-moning him back to a life fuller than the one he'd lost. For if, as was almost certain, the Catherine who had written him was also Robert's Catherine, then all their lives were linked.

By dusk his nerves were pitched to a key of high anticipation—and anxiety too. Nicholas and Jean might turn out to be useless. He might never know if the woman who had pressed her naked body against him was the same Catherine. He thought of cancelling the supper and abandoning the whole idea. But no! It was crucial not to hesitate, crucial to live this sequence by stages. To strengthen his control, he began a series of yoga exercises. And when, an hour later, becalmed, he jumped under the shower, he felt a fierce sense of purpose, like an athlete readying for a match with an opponent who would push him to the limit but which with an extraordinary effort he could still just win.

To sustain his calm, he lit one of Jules's cigarettes. And then, with the first puff, the entire heroic charade vanished, it just dropped away. For a second, registering the violence of his mood swings, he wondered if he had gone mad and knew the thrill, half-pleasurable, of having therefore become more interesting. And then he was not amused, he was afraid. It was one thing to have been brushed by madness, another thing to be carried away by it and not to know it.

But what if it hadn't been the cigarette at all that had downed him? Suppose it had been precisely the accident of his lighting up in the instant of losing control that in fact had tempered his fall? Sanity, then, was never further off than the corner supermarket, depending on his timing.

But that was a big if. His taste for risk was growing inordinate.

He went upstairs, hunted up Michael's number, and dialed London. Hearing Jane's induplicably light tones, he cried out happily, "Ah, angel of mercy, the voice in the world I most want to hear."

"Paul! How wonderful. Are you coming then? You must be going mad there on your own. Do come. I insist, Michael insists. Wait, what's that? Even the children, without prompting, insist."

"You're irresistible. Yes, I'd love to come—soon. I'll look at my schedule."

Before he knew it, he had agreed to attend the new *Hamlet* at the National, in which the courtiers at Elsinore were dressed like Capone-style gangsters; yes, he said, he too longed to see the new Francis Bacons at the Tate; and to visit the Bookhams in their new cottage outside Basingstoke would make the weekend perfect. Pleased that in extremity he knew how to manage and get relief, he hung up, promising to call back with arrival particulars.

He enjoyed the mood of rationality rewon, but as Varda's

place came into view, he became seized by anxiety. The clarity that had made him call Jane was only a bit of unconscious sleight of hand, a stopgap to ward off the truth of his actual disturbing change. He knew he could not turn away, he would not stop, he wanted the adventure.

At Varda's, Nicholas and Jean were studying fabric samples. "Oh, there you are," murmured Nicholas without getting up. "About time too."

Paul made excuses.

"You know, Professor, you can't neglect your friends for weeks on end and then count on ceremony. It's undignified for us to have to discover what you're up to from Jules. The salt of the earth isn't famous for getting things straight. He said—let me make sure I get this right—you were as broody and fidgety as a pregnant ferret. He said you were not polite, that you were always there, but that you were also not really there in your skin. So what's going on?"

"Don't harry him so," said Jean. "Let Paul sit down before you start on him."

"What neat designs," said Paul. "What are they for? Are you stage-setting again?"

"Did you see that, Jean?" said Nicholas. "That was a subterfuge, a pure red-winged subterfuge. But, let's agree: a subterfuge, to be effective, has got to go unnoticed."

"I didn't mean it as a subterfuge," said Paul.

"My boy," said Nicholas, "when you get to be my age, the only thing that matters is subtlety. It's the real stake in the war between the ages, and it's not negotiable. And we older folk feel perfectly within our rights to set the stakes when it's war with the young—I mean those a little younger than ourselves."

"I get you. I be subtle, or I sing."

"Exactly," said Nicholas with a chuckle. He seemed to be enjoying himself, though he was obviously serious enough not to want his bluff, if indeed it were one, to be called.

"I bet you never threatened Margot this way."

"You're right, but she always made it clear that emotional blackmail wouldn't work with her."

Paul grimaced. He felt put down at not having been found reserved from the start, as someone to be reckoned with, but he was flattered by the concern behind Nicholas' inquisitiveness.

"Very well," he said. "But I warn you not to expect very much. I do have a secret—though it's nothing special."

"We'll be the judge of that."

"Jules is right, I haven't been myself. This place is taking me further and further away from myself. What's happened is simply that I cannot stand doing history." Paul took a breath. "I'm trying my hand at fiction."

"Fiction."

"Drafts. Toward a novel or novelized journal, perhaps. It's all exhilarating and extremely frustrating. It just ought to be easier than it is. I can write five lines of historical narrative, parse each sentence, get each one not flagrantly wrong, then let the paragraph stand and move on. But fiction, when is it ever right?"

Nicholas stared at him with a kind of loathing.

Jean asked, "What are you writing about?"

"Various kinds of solitary life—but it's obviously a little too close to the bone. There's my solitude, of course, such as it is; there's Flaubert's at Croisset and Kafka's on Alchemist Alley; but I do desperately want current models, new versions." He paused. "I must say that, following Margot's lead, I've begun to think a lot about Robert Coustrieu. Do you know him?"

Nicholas let his jaw fall and began shaking his head.

"I only know the little I've heard about him from Margot, but I can't help feeling he's my man." Paul had been counting on the allure, even for these two, of participating in the making of a novel. Even the author of Martinique romances, gathering dust beside stale M&M's at checkout counters—Paul had seen this—could fuel to a hot blaze the envy and interest of the others, who, in the presence of a "real writer," would twitter, feckless. Nicholas reddened and bent his head down over his curtain work. Jean smiled. "So you want to know all about Robert Coustrieu? Well, go and introduce yourself to him."

"Yes, but I could obviously use a little preparation."

"That could be a mistake. He's more legendary than real, and what you'd hear about him might give you the wrong idea. Everyone seems to have met him at some time or another. Let's say, he's not easy."

"Is his music any good?"

"It's highly considered, even in Paris. We once heard some

pieces played at the Salle Pleyel. It's a weird, dissonant music of course, violent but very moving. It gets to you—it's fragmented and it's intense, more challenging and overpowering than beautiful."

"Are there any tapes?"

"I really don't know."

Nicholas coughed and scrutinized his designs.

Paul pressed on. "Is there any good reason for him to hole up in Seillans?"

Jean looked at Nicholas before continuing. "Of course. He has the house from his aunt, dead now but once a grand, eccentric lady." Jean thought for a moment. "She also lived alone. I realize now it's family tradition. His Aunt Marguerite was never really part of the social life of old Seillans, but from time to time she'd surface to run a civic affair with an iron hand. She ran the annual *aïoli*, and she got the most unlikely types to cook up vats of *rascasso* and tubers according to the old recipes. Then she'd drink the first glass, complain of the heat and crowds, and march off with her stick and parasol."

"A great old dame," said Nicholas, "a hero during the war, active in the Resistance; she bribed the Germans to release the local leader of the Maquis with her one and only bar of solid gold."

"Was Robert involved in any of this?"

"No, he was too young," said Jean. "He'd been sent down to spend the war with her. He used to go to the little church school. He learned his Latin from the village priest. He speaks Italian: the priest is Italian. I guess he used to visit his aunt in the years he was growing up, but I never ran across him then. The trouble with Robert is that you can't get any of the information directly."

"He's certainly been around for the last ten years," Nicholas added, holding up his designs to the disappearing light. "He's a great brooder, a wild man, but I suspect that his stance is mostly pose, or else he's sulking over the woman or two who've left him, deservedly, or some snub forgotten by everyone but him. I find his histrionics a huge bore."

"That's too judgmental, Nick," said Jean.

"Well, I've heard his music, so I know he has no talent. And he certainly has no personal style."

"Why do you say that?" asked Paul quietly. He did not want to unsettle the precarious mood.

"You're thinking of the exhibit, Nick?" said Jean.

Nicholas frowned. "I once agreed to have my designs exhibited in Seillans. I didn't like the idea at all, but since it was a charity and crippled children were involved, I couldn't refuse. Coustrieu, it turned out, had been asked to audition his music and apparently had gone into convulsions at the prospect."

"Convulsions?"

"Of laughter."

Paul felt a flash of fear.

"So he was invited to the opening along with the local elite. To no one's surprise, apparently—except my own—he turned up in an African explorer's costume, played his rubbish, drank and talked obsessively, never looked at the designs, and finally crashed into Mme. de Marly and bore her off like a prize."

"Who's that?"

"The organizer's catch," said Jean. "She'd come up from Cannes, had bags of money, and was expected to contribute. Except she went away with Robert before the time came to make pledges, and no one saw her again that season."

"Robert's had a lot of success with women?"

"What?" said Nicholas. "Because of Madame d' Em? Don't make me laugh. Of course, Catherine was another matter." Nicholas smiled and put down his drawings. "Damned attractive, dark, good figure, very bright. What she was doing wasting her time with Coustrieu is beyond me. She's a good twenty years younger and a serious painter herself—good family, good Paris connections, money."

"Catherine is a treasure," said Jean. "I've known her since she came here as a girl. Her grandmother was a great rival of Robert's aunt. Those were two fierce old ladies—I'd like to be as fierce when I'm seventy. Catherine's grandmother had the advantage of being rich but the disadvantage of being a foreigner. Not just Parisian, I mean. Was she actually Belgian, Nick, or was it just her husband? I'm not sure."

"I don't know," said Nick. "I'd rather not even think about the Belgian spirit afoot in Seillans. Excuse me." He heaved himself out of the deck chair and swaggered into the house.

Paul sat very still. He felt a cramp in his belly, leaving him as breathless as if he'd been hit a low blow. To Jean he was able to grunt, "Robert—how old is he—fiftyish?"

"Yes, about that—a little younger: mid-forties, I'd think."

"Do you happen to know if Catherine's grandmother's name was Lavernier?"

"Yes, it was something like that. Wait. No, wasn't it Demeunier? Where's Nick? He'll know."

Paul said rapidly, "Her son is Catherine's father? Catherine's name is Demeunier?"

"No, it's her daughter who's Catherine's mother; she lives in Brussels. I don't know her married name."

"So Catherine's name could be Lavernier."

Jean looked strangely at him.

"She's dark—she's intelligent, right, very fluent, has political interests."

"Yes," said Jean slowly.

Paul nodded. "I see."

Nicholas came back. Paul couldn't react. He felt seasick on solid ground.

He sat in the deck chair and let the conversation pass over and around him. Whatever its tenor—and it was mordant—the mere sound of human voices in his mood was beneficial. Nicholas and Jean were speaking of old women with exaggerated wills to power: Nicholas rumbled while Jean chewed pistachios and laughed. With a huge effort, as if he were drugged or drunk but struggling to make an impression of lucidity, Paul dredged up a suitable story of his grandmother in Paris: of how she'd dominated his summers with the high culture he'd begun to fear. The memories of those Julys—for a long time hated, afterward long suppressed—now came rising up in him, vivid, and he seized on them with gratitude, painting for his hosts the image of his sullen self, properly dressed, dragged from one airless museum to another, needing to satisfy the requirements of an order called "culture." And meanwhile he'd longed for one thing only: to be back in America with his friends, practicing driving and diving and sailing and picking up girls and what to do with them. He finished with a manic flourish, acting out the anguish of the first day in school when, during sports, after class, he exposed his sunken, "European" pigeon chest.

Jean laughed. "Ah, but it's not so sunken now."

"No," said Paul, "it's been inflated by the mistral."

Nicholas and Jean returned volubly to his theme, commiserating at the rigors to which parents subject their children in the name of the unintelligible thing that will one day stand them in good stead. Encouraged now, Paul told about his father's attempts to train him in the wily, cold, and vaunting mentality of the trader as part of a compulsory rite of passage. He described their Saturday morning sessions on Borum Place—with each word he felt the anger rise inside him—as he pitted against each other father and son, the adolescent spewing cocky invective at "capitalism," the man defending, as more than necessary, as right, the real ways of the market, the ways of business, adding always that he must never let the fact that his mother had been French—he stressed the past perfect—allow him to think that France could educate him to a mastery of modern life. Food, perhaps, chitchat and couture—métiers which, of course, were not to be discountenanced but which for all practical purposes. . . .

Later in the evening, Paul sat with Nicholas and Jean in their warm kitchen, energized by wine and the odd salutary memory of his childhood. Pretending to busy himself with a desert pear, he murmured, "By the way, you never told me. Are Robert and Catherine still together?"

Nicholas looked up, and Jean put a *crottin* on his plate. "Here, Nick," he said, "this one's a beauty." He smiled at Paul. "No, it's all over now, it's been over for almost a year. I don't know anything definite about the breakup, though Clara used to talk about it occasionally."

Suddenly Nicholas banged the stone handle of his fork onto the plate. "What the hell is all this fascination with Coustrieu anyway?" Nicholas glared at Paul. "You don't even know the man, so don't give me this crap about writing a novel." Nicholas forced a smile. "Why are you so interested?"

Paul blamed himself for having forgotten Nicholas' aggressiveness; he'd been caught unawares. What now? He wasn't eager to tell them about his night with Catherine. That was only part of it, anyway, only a thin eggshell container of the truth. He struggled to focus onto the moment his obsession—Margot Robert Catherine. All right, why was he so interested? He shook his head. "I'll tell you a few things. I was at Clara and Patrice's the other day: they mentioned Robert's visits and his slightly dangerous character. He's stuck in my mind, I'm curious." Paul watched Nicholas. He would have to be absolutely guarded. Nicholas had been piqued and would no doubt enjoy knowing something to his disadvantage. Paul shrugged, then half-laughed. "Gossip on an empty brain is strong drink."

Nicholas looked at him. Paul felt vexed: after all, he was in the right; the tendency to gossip raged unabated in these parts—a second mistral. And if a vice, it was evidently innocent enough to be flaunted by even a person as good as Clara. "I'm also a social scientist, Nick. And what else is social science except gossip quantified?"

"Oh, come on, Professor," Nicholas snorted, "you can do better than that."

"Nicholas!" said Jean.

Paul lifted up his hands: "What do you want to hear? Give me a clue."

"You can damn well stop playing so meek and holy. A man of your quality has no business going around picking at rumors. Look at you. The first time you came here you had us going on the subject of Margot. And now are you all finished with her? At least your being interested in her makes a bit of sense: you do live in her house. But Coustrieu—for God's sake. A novel? What rubbish!"

Paul was on the verge of answering vehemence vehemently—to what end? Breaking with them? What would Margot say? And the reason: information gathering on Robert and Catherine? She hadn't wanted him even to mention Catherine. "All right," Paul said, "if the stakes are so high." But he would not give Nicholas too easy a victory. "I'll level with you, but I'll tell you that your quarrel is not with me, it's with Robert Coustrieu."

"That's possible," said Nicholas calmly. "To the matter, sir."

"A few weeks ago I met Catherine in Seillans. Of course at the time, I didn't know who she was. I liked her a lot, she evidently liked me. She stayed at the house—with some other friends. Please, this is confidential."

"Yes, yes, my boy." Nicholas signed charity and understanding.

"Then she disappeared. I thought about finding her again, of course, but I didn't really know where to look. Then Margot linked the name Catherine to Robert and I started to wonder. But until I came here tonight I didn't really know that the two women are the same. I admit, I came hoping you would tell me this without my letting on why. The fact is she's almost certainly dropped me—so it's not something pleasant I want to talk about."

"I'm sorry," said Jean.

"No," said Paul, "This is all very helpful. I see now she would have been carrying her memories of Robert with her that night at La Casaubade."

"I hadn't realized that Catherine was back this summer," said Jean. "She's certainly kept a low profile." He looked puzzled. "I'm surprised she treated you so badly. Of course, we haven't had much contact with her since her grandmother died, and that's about the time she took up with Robert. At any rate, she seemed the very soul of decency. I'm shocked she should have changed so much."

"Feminism," said Nicholas. "In my day no respectable woman would have treated a man like that." He looked amused.

Paul smiled back, remembering Catherine's letter.

"What are you two grinning about?" said Jean.

"Jean's right," Nicholas continued. "She's a direct, thoughtful, instinctively tactful young woman. But of course: she became involved with Coustrieu. What could the outcome be except feelings of confusion and resentment? You, my boy, are Coustrieu's scapegoat."

Paul did not relish the phrase. "So when did she and Robert break up?"

Jean said, "She came down from Paris late last summer with the plan of staying for a few months. I don't know where she was staying, but you'd see her shopping at the market or drinking coffee at the *pâtisserie*. But then, before Christmas, she was gone again."

"But last Christmas isn't really our concern," said Nicholas. "We're talking about the future, aren't we? So what are you going to do? I assume from the fact that we're talking about her that you're still interested."

Paul nodded slowly.

"Well, you're right to be. I don't believe in the change. She's sure of herself, certainly every bit as strong as Coustrieu, and bound to have come to her senses."

This turn of conversation, too, did not particularly suit Paul. He did not want to rush anything with Catherine. He'd write her a note and attempt to produce a civil tone between them. Catherine had left Seillans the same time as Margot and as abruptly! Was that the link? Could they have left together? His heart began to race, but he tried to answer reasonably: "No, I think I'm just going to forget about her. She's a million miles away, and I haven't come to France for a liaison."

"Come on, Paul," said Jean, "give Catherine another chance. She's probably regretting you bitterly. What have you got to lose? You're not going to feel worse than you do right now, right?"

"Right now, I would as soon forget about her and enjoy the pleasure of your company."

"Isn't that nice," said Nicholas.

Paul knew what he was avoiding. The subject of Catherine was bound to produce from him his set speech on the behavior of lovers, drawn from personal experience and enriched with literary examples and wisdom sentences. This was a speech he'd already delivered countless times in the bars, restaurants, living rooms, and movie lobbies of New York, where a general hypertrophy of self-absorption had spawned a culture of effusiveness and litigation, in which everyone was ready to lay out before everyone else protocols of his or her relationships, acting at once as plaintiff, accused, prosecutor, and member of the higher court, and where the hapless listener risked abuse for some casual failure to supply the requisite agreement. It was unlikely that Nicholas and Jean would respond in kind, but it was not something he wanted them to do. From what they had so far offered him in the way of analysis, it was clear they had a mercifully weak interest in sociobiology. In fact, there was only one way in which Nicholas and Jean could help: they could give him the information he wanted—and a lot more of it than what they'd given—but for this he would have to be patient.

Instead they discussed Nicholas' and Jean's Christmas plans (they were going skiing near Chamonix), and Paul soon left to set off up the road. He was eager to think over the news, but he was also exhausted by the strain involved in gathering it. It was as if his mind were trapped in a mineshaft, needing directions from its rescuers.

Suddenly he stopped and listened, straining. Instinct made him turn off his flashlight and scramble up the slope. The sound of voices and laughter filled the darkness, and around the corner, on the road immediately ahead of him, he could see tiny, flickering, shifting lights. A group of figures, made grotesque by their shadows, came stamping and lurching down the road. Who were they? What were they doing? There was no other house further up. As they passed below him, he saw by the light of a swinging kerosene lamp their tawdry clothes—tattered and filthy—their tea-colored skin and mangled feet. There were a dozen of them, men and women—and a pack of verminous dogs, one of them a pit-bull, a Raggedy Ann doll clamped in its jaws—moving in a group, arms and hands casually linked. Their speech was a jumble: they all seemed to be talking, howling, and laughing drunkenly at once, and someone was singing a Hungarian song. In a few minutes the darkness engulfed them, and he was alone with the cicadas and his shock.

At home, although there were no visible signs, he knew they had been on the terrace, peering in through the doors at the living room lit by the small lamp he had turned on before leaving.

Chapter Eight

Paul was performing the rites of the newly arisen: having quartered an orange and sliced some Brovès bread for toast, he was now grinding frozen Arabian coffee beans. He was moving quickly: the morning was almost gone, but he intended to visit the farm that Margot and Liz Wainwright had recommended for its goat cheese, honey, and rosé. As he poured boiling water, he heard the sound of tires braking on the gravel. He looked out: the car had a blue light on its roof. Two police officers in kepis were emerging on the terrace, incongruous in their dark uniforms against the bright hills.

"You are Monsieur van Pein?"

Paul let them in. The younger officer announced that they had come from the prefecture in Grasse.

"Grasse?" Paul stared at him.

"Yes, Monsieur." The older man was glancing about the living room with a look of distaste, his hands behind his back. "In matters of such gravity, Seillans does not have competence, and we are called in." The younger officer, raw but evidently an athlete of some arcane art of self-defense, was practicing politeness.

"What is this matter of gravity?"

Neither answered.

The older officer settled himself into the rattan-bottomed chair, then said, in a heavy, grunting voice that alluded to unplumbed reserves of authority: "Just after midnight last night, you left the house of Monsieur Nicholas Varda. Is that correct?"

"Yes."

"Describe your movements from this point on."

"What do you mean? I came home."

"Yes, go on."

"What is there to say? I walked home."

"You made no detour of any kind?"

"No, of course not. What is this all about?"

"You will be good enough to tell us what you saw and heard while walking home."

"Nothing," Paul said.

"Nothing? Nothing at all? You heard no sounds?"

"No, not really."

"Nothing of a suspicious nature, nothing unusual in any way?"

"What can I tell you?" said Paul. His heart was racing, but he took his impulse as right. His impressions were not for everyone, let alone a foreign police. "I heard a dog barking from down below in the valley, and I saw a small animal, probably a badger, dart across the road as I came toward the house. Look, what is this all about?"

"You will be informed. And the lights? You saw no lights?"

"No."

"None of any kind? No car lights?"

"No. There are no more houses up here; there's almost never any traffic except for the mailman's car. Well?"

The officer nodded to the younger man.

"After you left Monsieur Nicholas Varda last night, a group of vagrants attempted to break into his house, although it was plain that Monsieur Varda and his companion were at home. Monsieur Varda produced a hunting rifle which he aimed at the intruders, and when, according to the plaintiff, the vandals answered his warning with derisive laughter, he shot one of them in the calf, whereupon the group fled, carrying the wounded person with them."

"My God!" said Paul. "Did one of them actually accuse Nicholas of shooting?"

"No." The older policeman picked up a cup and poured some coffee.

Paul gestured to the other, who shook his head.

The older man said: "This group appeared at Monsieur Varda's house a quarter of an hour after you'd left, and yet you, Monsieur, are certain you did not hear a thing."

"That's right, I told you."

The young officer said, "We believe this group was observing the house of Monsieur Varda from the road for some time before attempting to enter. This would have been the same time you went up the road."

"I'm sorry, I can't help you."

"In that case . . . ." The older man got up and stood looking at him.

Paul said, "What did they want with Varda and Jean? Do you know?"

"There have been a number of such incidents recently," said the young officer. "Burglary does not appear to be the motive, although in some cases valuable objects have been taken. This group aims at intimidating its victims. The residents of our community are growing alarmed; we therefore ask visitors of all nationalities to assist us in clearing up this matter."

The older officer said, "It's a gang of foreigners."

Paul smiled. "Are you quite sure?"

The young man said, "We French have various failings, but aimless violence is not one of them."

Paul smiled. "But that's just a deduction and surely not an argument?"

The older man grimaced and shook his head slowly. "We will be the judge of the rules of evidence, Monsieur." He walked up close to the tapestry. "A nice house you have." He turned. "How long have you been here?"

"A few months. It belongs to Madame Stevens."

"Ah, yes, the American woman. And you're an American too?"

"Yes."

"Your passport, please."

"What for?"

"You will be informed," said the officer.

"If you insist. It's upstairs."

The older officer watched him steadily. On the landing,

Paul hesitated for a moment and turned to hear what they were saying, but they were muttering. He moved hurriedly to the study, where he rifled through the papers on his desk. He felt flustered and more guilty, perhaps, than was appropriate. But—damn it!—he'd only miscalculated, thinking that denying what he'd seen would be the prudent thing. It was misconceived implicit loyalty. He continued to push aside piles of papers and to open and shut the drawers of the desk. Then, as he was raking the bottom drawer, he felt wedged in against the plywood partition at the back an envelope forgotten or lost. Tugging it out, he saw, written in a flowing hand, Margot's address. There was a letter inside. He stuffed it into the pocket of his bathrobe. Finally, in a drawer to the right, he found his passport under the aerograms.

The older officer slowly turned the pages of the passport, then closed it in his hands. "You have no residence permit."

"I'm sorry, no. I forgot to apply for it. But I can get one at the mayor's office, can't I?"

"You'd better, at once. Otherwise your stay is highly irregular. I realize you're an American, but it just so happens that in France you will have to obey our rules." He dropped the passport on the kitchen table. They turned to leave. Paul fingered the envelope in his pocket. The young officer said, "If on reviewing the incidents of last night, you discover that you did indeed see or hear something unusual, be sure to contact us."

"I certainly will."

The older man said, "That goes for anything you see and hear in the future."

Paul shrugged them off. He watched them march across his terrace and get into their Citroën. Comedians! They were just playing hardboiled: there was nothing they could charge him with. It was Varda's fault for having put them on his trail.

As they started their engine, he pulled out the letter. On a page covered with tiny squares were only a few words:

M., I won't forget. The risk and closeness—ours alone, and all the other nights, the horror of those endless nights—they will be with me forever, and so we are bound together.

C.

Paul looked at the envelope again. He could make out the local postmark, but the date was smudged. "C," of course, was Coustrieu. Oh my God, "C" was Catherine! Could that possibly be Catherine's hand? Of course, it could be. He had only to compare it with her handwriting. But her previous letter had been typewritten, and the note she'd left him after the first night he'd mislaid. He railed against himself for his carelessness.

If he knew where she lived, he could write her a letter and hope for a reply, which in the worst possible case would be a handwriting sample. His heart began to race as he asked Paris Information for the phone number and address of Catherine Lavernier.

The operator paused and said, "I have no party in Paris under that name."

"Ridiculous," said Paul. "I know she's in the book. She probably lives somewhere in St. Germain."

The operator was obstinate.

"Oh, never mind." He would figure it out some other way. He knew he'd copied out her Seillans number from her first letter. He ran upstairs to ransack his reading notes, found it on a wine-stained sheet of ruminations on the calf's head in *Sentimental Education*, and dialed the number.

It was no longer in service.

He drank coffee, brooding over the fact that Catherine had not been listed in the Paris phone book. Suddenly he remembered: Catherine had rented her house from the mayor, a famous Communist. Although uneasy from his earlier brush with the cops from Grasse, Paul phoned the mayor's office. But Friday was his honor's day at home on the rue des Nains.

"I'm sorry to disturb you, *Monsieur le maire*, but the matter is urgent."

M. Noircet said something disobliging.

"A young woman stayed in a house you found for her last summer—Catherine Lavernier. Could you give me her address in Paris?"

There was a grunt, then silence.

Paul had to repeat most of this, finally shouting, "It's important: Catherine Lavernier—a dark woman, a painter. She came with American friends—Ellen and Alan!"

Half turning from the phone, Noircet let loose a squall of incomprehensible dialect—it sounded like Basque—until Paul recognized the formulaic epithet displaying the benevolent fraternal character of the speaker—*imbecile*—then *conard* and in the same tonality *amèricain*. Furious, Paul could only repeat himself. Noircet insisted on referring to Catherine's surname as L'Inconnu until handing over the phone to his wife. Paul repeated the drill, keeping away from the name Lavernier. In a pinch he would allude to his friendship with the postmaster. Finally, the woman produced a Paris address and phone number, calling Paul *jeune homme* and raucously wishing him luck of the chase.

The address was an omen. Catherine lived on the Rue Thénard, almost immediately next to the Hôtel Collège de France, where Nina had stayed when she'd first come to Paris as a medical student. In Hampstead Paul had seen a photograph of her taken in front of the hotel.

He gulped coffee. What did it mean that both the mayor and Paris Information had not recognized Catherine's surname? Had she seen through Paul's disguise and in a gesture of complicity disguised herself? Or was more at stake, and was she was hiding from the real Robert? This idea made her even more appealing. He would write to her as soon as he had thought things over carefully, indeed, thought each of them over carefully in turn—Margot, Robert, now Catherine! At last, knowing this was precisely what he could not do in his state— it would all have to settle or else be seen from a distance—he told himself to get more information. He would need a sample of Robert's handwriting. Remembering the misfortune at Varda's, he perceived he had a condolence call to pay.

The door was open. He felt hardly noticed in the crowd. Off in one corner Nicholas was surrounded by half the expatriate community, drinks in hand. His cheeks were flushed; Paul saw him make the gesture of raising and then lowering a rifle and then bursting into laughter. Jean rushed by carrying more drinks; he looked grim and responded only distractedly to Paul's expressions of concern.

Finally he succeeded in cornering Jean. "I know this could sound perfectly mad, but did you ever get a letter from Robert Coustrieu?"

"What about?" asked Jean, with some anxiety.

"It's not important what it's about. You remember my plan, I'm writing about solitaries—I know this might not be the moment for it—but I need to see his handwriting."

Jean thought. "I have something," he said. "The time he complained about my singing."

Paul said, "Could I see it?"

"What, now?"

Paul nodded.

"With all these people?"

"Please," said Paul. "Here, give me the tray, I'll take it around for you. See if you can lay hands on it for a second and show me."

Jean returned from the bedroom with a page of Robert's screed. Paul seized it. It looked familiar—but not entirely familiar. It could or could not be "C." He had to give it back. Catherine could have written the note.

He wanted to leave but he could not so soon, so he stationed himself in the corner of the living room opposite Nicholas and beside his gunrack. To his surprise he heard Margot's name being mentioned alongside him. A tall, gray-haired woman, her skin leathery from the sun, was saying, "I remember when Margot Stevens had an intruder last year—it was just some drunken vagrant actually—but I heard that she scared him off good and proper. I've always thought I'd never want to get on her wrong side."

"I once asked her if she was related to the Boston Stevens," said her companion, "and she cut me dead, though apparently she is the daughter of old Stevens. And a couple of years ago in Newport her name came up; there'd been a scandal." She lowered her voice. "Margot had an illegitimate daughter who was raised by the parents."

"Margot with a child? Somehow that's hard to imagine."

"Yes, but aren't there a lot of things about our Margot which one has to imagine!" The woman turned suddenly and stared at Paul, who was stroking the waxy handle of a rifle while pretending to be absorbed in a gun magazine at an adjacent table. He lowered his head and walked away. So there was Margot's daughter to think about. Was she also a "C"? She could be eighteen or so—and her name? He saw Margot's naked thighs and belly and her infant daughter laid across them, then looked up into the advancing smile of Liz Wainwright. He shrank. "Paul," she said, "have you been following all this? Isn't it terrible?"

Paul nodded, but he wasn't inclined to think that he would have very much insight from her into the bohemian raid. He smiled. "You know I was just thinking of you. I'm on my way to that farm you mentioned."

"With the marvelous goat cheese and wine? Are you actually going now? Paul, you can do me a great favor."

She wanted him to stop off with her at her house, which was on the way, and take a flagon and a basket and bring her back some wine and cheese. He agreed to follow her car.

As he drove he realized he could unearth a good bit more on Margot by finding out about the Stevens of Boston. This was exciting. He would write to Tammy. In graduate school they had prepped each other for their qualifying exams—she studying only to bide her time before entering her father's investment firm, he resisting that fate with the same irrational stubbornness. As he remembered their evenings together— quizzing each other, tense and bleary-eyed—he thought how strenuous those days had seemed then and how simple, now, in retrospect.

When he followed Liz into the semidarkness of her *mas*, the phone was ringing. "It's from America, Paul. Give me a few minutes."

He wandered around the room until he found himself at a small writing desk under the window, where amid a clutter of bills and brochures, he spied a familiar handwriting. It was impossible for him not to scan at least the visible script. His entire adolescence had been an object lesson in the importance of gathering information not necessarily destined for his eyes. Reading the letters between his mother and grandmother had helped avert some of their more nefarious designs on his leisure. Forewarned was forearmed. In front of him now was something of considerable interest: Margot was responding to news from the Wainwrights. His need was overpowering, and on deftly turning over the letter, he saw his own name leap from the page. He was dumbfounded. Margot was complaining of not having heard from him and asking the Wainwrights to give her news of him. Feeling puzzled, elevated, and also a little betrayed, he dropped the letter just as Liz was coming toward him with her flagon and basket. They chatted, then Paul said: "Have you had any news of Margot? I haven't heard from her in a while."

"Oh yes, we just got a letter yesterday. She's in England you know and was apparently in Scotland and not alone. I get the impression she was there with a man. It would be nice for her not to be alone. She's such a lovely person, you know, and so intelligent and kind. Unusual too. She has that way of being with you and not, but I never mind, not with her."

The farm was halfway down the valley, hidden in the curve of a hill, in a scene tranquil until he drove through the gate. Then a couple of scroungy Afghans came staggering stiff-legged up to him, not knowing whether to treat him as enemy or customer. A bunch of chickens, confused by the racket, scrambled in all directions—one rushing between his legs, clucking, its neck stretched forward, feet moving staccato. An old woman appeared, dressed in black, followed by a skinny girl in a thin dress with a mop of blond curls, pouting a little—deprived, perhaps, of the glory of dealing with the customer. The old woman led Paul to a shed among the bleating goats—there must have been fifty of them—and pointed down shadowy stairs to a cool, dank, stone chamber, where the cheeses lay pale and secluded on shelves of fine wire mesh. The girl followed him down the stairs and stood beside him, watching, speaking only when he turned to ask about the differences in color; for some were chalky white, others cream-colored, others yellow and less unctuously rounded.

"It's the age, M'sieur. Pointing to the firm, shadowy ones, she said, "Those are the ripest. Take the ones you like, it's a matter of preference," and she held out a small wooden basket lined with grape leaves.

His movements slowed by the hush, he drifted from rack to rack and in the dank voluptuousness felt again his craving for a deep, green peace—his oasis, his garden ecstasy, a refuge from the torture of identity. He thought he heard again Robert's music the night in Seillans, just before Catherine had appeared among the fountains. Swaying to the music in the musky smell, the bleating of the goats blurred to a murmur by the thickness of the walls, he struggled to drift inward to that phantom place.

He smiled at the girl with a remote, exalted love and handed the basket back. "You choose for me," he said. Startled, she reached swiftly from shelf to shelf until she had piled up a half dozen cheeses on the leaves. "Go on," he said. "I'll come up in a minute."

Alone, he could feel the green place drifting further away, and not to have to experience its entire loss, he followed the girl up the stairs, through the goat sheds, and out into the court-yard in the brilliant sun, amid the cackle of chickens and the yapping of the Afghans, who rushed at him again. The girl stood across the way, scolding two small children in dirty smocks, and the old woman sat on a broken chair outside her kitchen. "Some honey?"

He nodded.

"Some rosé and perhaps some eggs?"

The woman went to the kitchen table, moistening with her lips the end of a pencil stub and adding up the charges. "*Voilà*," she said and pushed the piece of brown paper across the table. Staggered by the padded bill, Paul paid silently. As he drove back along the winding roads, he thought how well the woman had known what she was doing. After the descent into the goat cellar, visitors would pay double for the romance of buying straight from the farm. He was sorry not to have let her know he knew this and knew, too, that behind the crumbling walls and primitive sheds stood sleek chrome and steel machinery.

At La Casaubade, at least, the chrome and steel machinery of Margot's will was unconcealed.

To strengthen his forces, he made a detour for a restaurant north of Seillans, where he ordered the *repas rabelaisien.*

Tastes are marrying on my tongue—salmon and sorrel, cream and champagne: I am having an orgasm of tastes. Suppose I were sharing this meal with Margot. My ecstasy would be dissipated. A meal is as exacting as a spy or a lover—an insistent body of sensations requiring concentration or praise.

An elaborate dish of veal and morels.

This blank for bliss.

Damn, here come roasted goat cheese and a flan of passion fruit already: I'm being killed with plenty. I complain to the serving girl, and now she's hurt and everything's out of control. I have to struggle to find my vein again.

So I am taking up pen in hand to write: "Tastes are marrying on my tongue: salmon and sorrel and cream and champagne . . . ." I call this the work of recomposition.

The Work of Recomposition

Everything is these two things only—the beginning of bliss and the certainty of its rupture, the eternally repeated moment of broken trust. And so the work of recomposition tries to turn this interrupted bliss into another thing—into thought, into quite another curious thing.

The waitress is coming back, having misinterpreted my smile. I keep the peace by praising what she hands me: a tulip glass of wild strawberries buried in snowy tarragon sherbert.

My thought began in struggle. It has always been a matter of reasoning one's way out of pain, of fleeing from the threat of loss, until one's found the amazing surplus—radical gaiety, the gay science of inventing masks.

The bill arrives in the hollow of a disemboweled, morocco-bound treatise. I lift the lid; it plays a serenade, worth recording: *Eine kleine Nachtmusik*, performed by *Theologiae Fundamentalis Reinerding Seminario Fuldensi Praepositi, 1864*. The meal is a Total Work of Art. The bill is grandiose too—I pay.

How much is this ceremony of wine and writing worth? Margot makes it possible by belonging to my life. She pulls me, she is occupied with me. But how good is a bliss made possible only by her absence?

Paul got up, gathered his things, and walked out to his car, which was the last one parked on the gravel beneath the three milky globes of a wrought-iron lamp. Leaning over the fender, he opened his notebook and continued writing:

I say, like hunger there is need for love. And as in times without hunger one imagines oneself starving, in times of love one imagines oneself abandoned. That is worse than any feeling of a loss that could be named. It is the anxiety that will not let me live but if canalized will let me write.

He closed his book and got behind the wheel. Spider, spider of autonomy, spinning out of nothing—writing—a durable web, a web in which one lives? doesn't, cannot live! Enviable Bruno, enviable spider.

Suddenly the thought elated him that dependency wasn't the point anymore. He should not underestimate what he'd achieved. Margot was spying on him; in a deeper, more interesting sense she had become his correspondent. The words he had spun into his notebook were more than the Work of Recomposition; they were notes for his best yet letter to Margot. Not now, of course—she was not ready for so much knowledge of him. But it would all finish in a letter. The prospects for such writing were glorious.

Glancing down beside him, he saw on the front seat Liz Wainwright's empty flagon and basket, and the effect of the orgy began to drain away. As he drove along the empty road he realized the strength he took from wine and writing was inferior to Margot's. She was nourished by a life unknowably bigger than his. Stop and reflect: Margot alongside Robert—Margot tangled with Catherine—Margot giving birth to her daughter: all Margot's passionate nights. But this Margot, too, was hungry for news of him—of him. He would send her another mask. He went to his desk, spread out her letter, and studied it until, exhausted from the effort to own her memory of Pacific nights, he fell asleep.

Chapter Nine

Hi Paul,

So you've landed in the South of France, you lucky chunk. I don't know when I'll have any vacation again, so I keep alive the memory of a perfect summer night on the Delaware. But once the flowcharts start multiplying and meetings drag on past dinnertime, I need headier fare. So Anna and I will be spending a week on dear old Guana this Christmas: I want to feel stroked and coddled and move in slow motion. Anna will keep me from total torpor with short talks on Simonides, the *mater*'s phallus, and so forth.

I'm kind of busy, so I'll get to the point: your Margot Stevens. This took some doing, since I don't have immediate access to her exalted circles, though I still have a few spies left over from Miss Porter's, and Gloria is assistant head of research at *Time*. Daffy proved the most resourceful, so here's as much of the story as I could uncover.

Your Margot was adopted by the Stevens when she was a tyke of seven or eight—pretty and bright and no doubt considered a good deed. The Stevens were then in their fifties— very rich, with a mansion near Fenway Park—connoisseurs and collectors (specialty: Ch'ing bronzes). I have no idea how she fared there, but you can read in an old copy of the *Globe* that she was engaged at nineteen to a tall, dark foreigner with musical

107

abilities—the rogue son of a noble family from Roussillon. Draw
your own conclusions. The Stevens ran true to type—formalists
in social matters, unamused by outsiders. We couldn't find Margot's wedding announcement, but it seems she became pregnant soon thereafter. Her beau was put to work in Stevens'
Savings & Loans, and they must have made a striking, if somewhat off-putting young couple, awaiting the birth of their
daughter Catarina and the legitimation of the eligible.

Mummy and Daddy, in love with their granddaughter, hid
their chagrin, putting up the young family in a carriage house on
Byewood, whence Margot started life again as a Radcliffe girl
(with advanced standing).

Well, an anthropological education gives a girl with wild
ideas still wilder ones, and soon she was tearing through Cam-
bridge, doing fieldwork with a crowd whom the Stevens did not
care for at all. Predictably, she left her adoptive class. In those
circles that is not so easy, but deals are always possible: Margot
left without her daughter and evidently without waiting, either,
to legitimize her fiancé. There was a good deal of talk: Heiress
Leaves Baby, Age One, was not an everyday headline even in
the seventies. The grandparents, says Gloria, raised the girl
with all the love that Margot never felt for them.

Catty Stevens, now Wren, is a graduate student in art history, married to a lawyer-acquaintance of Peggy's who works out
of Brussels: Catty is charming and quite correct but maybe a *bit*
of a prig. What else? Her father, of course, the foreign gentle-
man with artistic inclinations, faded out, certainly well-
remunerated, and even Margot (they say) had some money due
to her that couldn't be taken away. There the story ends, as far
as my informants know. I personally checked out her Radcliffe
records—she began a doctoral program in anthropology at Har-
vard but never finished.

By the way, everyone was intrigued by my questions but
confused by my motives. I was vague—how could I be otherwise: you've left me in the dark. Paul, are you in love with this
woman? Write soon.

Tammy

There had been a letter from Margot in the very same
delivery. Just as Tammy's letter reminded him that he was spying on her, Margot's letter confirmed his belief that she was
spying on him.

November 25

Dear Paul,

I was amazed to receive a letter from Jean informing me that you have actually met Catherine, though you had not mentioned this fact to me. This, my friend, is less than rigorous. I am even more surprised that you have continued to keep silent on the subject. You know, of course, my view of her—at any rate you've had some indication of it, but this is hardly a warrant for deception—quite the opposite. Let us go back to the beginning. I would like you to write me the circumstances of your meeting. As you have not yet met Robert, or so you say, I presume that you did not meet her with him. Is it possible that they are together again? I must say that while I'm sorry she's around again, I can't say I'm not glad she's back.

It's time, really time, you met Coustrieu. Work at it: Clara and Patrice should be able to arrange a meeting.

First, though, do sit down and write to me, explaining in detail what has happened. Paul, I hope that in the future you will not conceal such information from me.

Margot

Very well, the gages were down. Paul was angry at Jean for having meddled. He had specifically asked them not to mention his meeting Catherine. Or was it possible that Margot had deliberately asked them to spy on him just as she had the Wainwrights? To judge from her letter, Jean hadn't told her much; probably his loyalties were divided. It might have been nothing more than a piece of mischief on Nicholas' part, who would enjoy getting Jean to provoke Margot. What did she want from him? Or was her deviousness simply second nature, a habit acquired in the refined salons of her youth, where indirection had been her sole device to elude the Stevens' will? Still, if she herself was not forthcoming, why wasn't she afraid that Robert would be—in ways that would damage her?

Yet Paul was glad that Jean had written to Margot: it seemed sure to speed the scene along. For the first time Margot was openly declaring Robert's importance, though Paul had known of it for weeks. The triangle once outside him now included him as Margot's proxy. In fact, there was now not one triangle but two—*at least* two: Paul noted this development with exultation. His life in France was becoming thick with future. He was impatient to join the configuration of the others. Margot was urging him into it, and he was willing to go.

Should he force her hand? To write her the truth of his evening with Catherine could prompt her to bring her strategy into the open. Catherine's humiliation would give Margot a pleasure hard to conceal. Whatever her relation to Catherine had been once, she hated her now. That, presumably, was why she'd been happy to learn that Catherine was still on the scene. Her hatred would have a vivid target.

His great surprise, however, was the strength of his desire to protect Catherine. He did not want to give Margot the satisfaction of knowing that only the spell she wove prevented him from pursuing her. As he imagined writing to Margot, he spun with excitement and trepidation. It was impossible not to write, but to do so would alienate her. His thoughts turned swiftly to Clara: she could champion his desire to get closer to Robert and perhaps even bring them together. Clara's affection made Margot's enmity easier to bear. He practically leapt for the telephone.

It was Patrice who answered, making him feel shy, almost guilty. Clara would have been able to half-formulate his desires: with Patrice he did not know how to ask for what he wanted. So he began by wondering how the new soffits were holding up.

"Splendidly, splendidly," said Patrice. "And thank you for your help with them. We've really been holed up here the last few weeks. Are you coming to see us again? I hope that's why you're calling. In fact we were just planning a break in the routine. What do you say to some shooting on Thursday?"

"I'd love to see you again," said Paul, "though I'm not sure about shooting. It's been some time since I've handled a gun. I think I'd better say no to that. But how do you feel about a visit another day soon?"

"Good idea! Come Friday and spend the night. I know that Clara will be pleased to see you. She's often spoken of you."

"That makes me very happy. Look, can I have your advice? In her letters Margot has continued to ask me if I'd met

Robert Coustrieu. I would like to meet him, but I don't know how to approach him. Do you think . . . ?"

"You mean ask him this weekend? Of course I could, it's the logical thing to do. Would that suit you?"

"It certainly would," said Paul. He would make his excuses to Michael and Jane.

Patrice said, "I'll do my best, but I can't promise he'll come. He can be quite stubborn about not doing what he doesn't want to."

"Don't go to any trouble; it's not that important."

"No problem. End of the day then on Friday."

Paul was giddy with affection for the person who'd allowed him to have his way. "Is there anything I can bring?"

"No, nothing. Just your good spirits."

"My very best regards to Clara."

"Of course. She'll be delighted. Well, *mon vieux* . . . ."

"May I ask if you've heard from Margot?"

"Not for a while. Clara's the letter writer in the family."

"Yes, it would be her bent exactly."

Patrice laughed. "I'm afraid I must go. We're about to leave for Grasse."

What if Robert didn't come? What if he did? The wait was going to be so long.

Friday came. Paul spent half the morning packing his rucksack, while Madame Onafaro set about her work slowly and deliberately, managing to get into every step of his way, which she excused with countless *pardon-monsieur*'s. Her awkwardness was due less to any fault of her own, he realized, than to his restless pacing through the house, as he sought out the right clothes, the right book, the bottle of Sauterne that he meant to take along, and finally the small erotic print—lots of green lines indicating the shadowy pudendum of a young girl whose hair was coiffed in the shape of a steer's head. He'd bought it in St. Paul but suddenly hated it, realizing that there was no one at Clara's he could possibly give it to. So he pressed it on the grateful but nonplussed Madame Onafaro, who certainly found it disgusting, pointing out regretfully that there was no room for it on the back of her bicycle: perhaps she could leave it with Monsieur until next time? She was sure her niece would like it; she liked paintings and had probably seen the original at the museum in Vence.

As Paul stubbornly went about warming up some cabbage soup for her, she settled on one of the chairs in the kitchen, rolling down her sleeves with concentration. Paul said, "And how did Madame compare at cooking up *garbure* for you, eh?"

The woman seemed stunned.

"I mean, how was it, working for her? Much easier than me, I bet." He had never had a conversation with her before; usually he went out for a walk or took the car to Draguignan on her day. He smiled. "I never seem to know what to ask you to do next."

"You're no trouble, Monsieur." She began to eat. "The soup is good." She lifted her spoon several more times and chewed her bread with application. "Madame wasn't any trouble either."

"But she must have had so many more guests than I. No one ever comes now."

She shrugged.

"No gentlemen callers?" Paul laughed.

She looked at him without changing her expression. "That is not for me to say, Monsieur," and she redoubled her concentration on the soup. The bowl half-empty, she got up, took it to the sink, emptied it, and bleakly washed it out. Of course, it was pointless to question her—she was not a gossip. Either she drew the line at the affairs of foreigners or else found it unseemly to talk of intimate things with someone not of her own class.

An hour later he was on the path, the rucksack high on the back of his neck. As he strode along, there began to dawn on him enough distance, enough of a sense of the ridiculous, to realize that he was certainly bound for disappointment. Robert would no doubt prove moody but also quite rough, and the story of his Catherine would turn out to have no real conclusion. At the same time, he lamented his own credulity in having allowed himself to be so sucked into the vortex of Margot's desires. When Michael had called that morning to ask why in the name of God he'd never bothered to tell them that he wasn't coming to London after all, he'd been appalled to be taken so completely by surprise—he'd forgotten his promise to call—and was afterward in awe, almost, of the extent to which everything outside Margot's fiction had become unreal for him.

As he approached their place, he spotted Clara on the *berge* below him, in a floppy hat, her basket over her arm, striding, then stopping, with a mixture of purpose and indecision, searching the ground. He dropped back behind a bramble bush to watch her easy, supple, full-breasted figure until she disappeared. Then he was stabbed by a feeling that was less sexual desire—indeed it was hardly sexual at all—than a sort of envy of her being. It pulled him toward her, he wanted to take it from her; and it drove him away, in admiration. He envied her serenity and boldness, the ease of her relationship with Patrice, the devotion and the inevitability of it; it was as plain and ripe as the meals they took together and as rare as the most delicate discovery. The weight of his sadness exhausted him. He suddenly felt very tired from the hike, not at all ready to move on to the next event, with barely enough strength even to stumble into a grassy hollow, where he fell back against a lush brake of ferns between two rocks and stretched his legs out, his hands crossed on his chest, unmoving. The warm sun shone obliquely on his face, he felt himself dropping into a drowse, oblivious for a second to everything but the high hum of the cicadas and the squawking of the jays, and then oblivious to everything.

The explosion of a rifle in the hills awakened him: he grabbed at his watch: he had been asleep for fifteen minutes. He walked toward the house half-dazed and full of a confusing sweetness. Rounding the last corner, he pulled back, this time behind the woodshed, for he saw the door of a grimy dark-blue Mercedes open and Patrice and Clara move toward it, shouting greetings. This would be Robert.

A tall man got out of the car—in an ironed blue shirt and tight black sweater, his beard neatly groomed, not at all the wild man Paul had expected. Paul stayed back, curious—and anxious.

They embraced and walked together under the tree to the wicker chairs where Paul had been the first time. Paul shook off the rucksack, moved to the other end of the shed, and sat down on a bench. As he dug his heels in and relaxed, they settled, and he could watch them and hear their voices easily.

Clara's laughter broke into the air. "Robert, you're a beast. It's no wonder you haven't got a single friend. So stop playing the misanthrope. I know it's all an act for Patrice's benefit."

"Yes," said Patrice. "You'll never convince us you're worse than you are."

Robert watched them, smiling, then began filling and lighting his pipe. "What's the scam? You never called me up before out of the blue with a specific date. But I bet I know what you're up to: you're counting on a dinner party from me in return."

Clara laughed. "I never make bad bargains, you know that."

Patrice said, "We'd like you to meet a friend of ours."

"What for?"

"Now that's a brilliant question," said Clara.

Patrice said, "Paul's an American professor, here on sabbatical. He's perfectly all right."

"American? I didn't know Club Med had bought into these hills."

Clara's voice became slow and husky. "He's very nice. We know him because he's staying at Margot's."

"Margot's?"

"He's rented La Casaubade for a year."

Paul thrust his body forward to stare. Robert was supposed to start off these visits slowly, but now he was shouting her name. "That's very interesting. So that's the game. The man's her spy, and you've asked him up to meet me."

"Robert, he is not."

"More trouble! So I'm not done with her yet." He got up and began pacing. "Come on, why is she renting the house? She never has before, right? It's not the money, I know her fairly well. And it's not to caretake the place. Jules is there, and that old queen Varda is sure to have his eye turned up the hill at all times."

"Robert, don't exaggerate. What harm would Margot ever want to do to you?"

"Wouldn't you like to know. She lost her soul in the New

Hebrides, and she's interested in replacing it. Yours will do, and yours, too."

"Yours, you mean."

Robert looked grim. "It's no joke, she makes me unhappy. You can't love her, you know. I've tried—and after all these years I can't and I won't."

"Oh, I've seen you both happy together."

Robert shrugged. "I can't stand her myths. She's some sort of Jungian, you know, though I think she just makes them up as she goes along. We've had Margot the Nurturer, Margot the Virgin, and Margot of the Long Memory. Now we have Margot the Vengeful—Goddess of the Hunt. What's her connection with this American, anyway? Is he her little animus, and is he supposed to do her feeling for her?"

"They've never even met."

Robert laughed and began refilling and lighting his pipe. "She'd like the challenge. I can see her warming to it: remote control."

Patrice said quietly, "What would she get from that?"

"From control? Yes, you're too good to know. Let's say she's curious about life in these parts and wants the information without any expense of soul."

"Why, is she planning something?"

"No, nothing in particular. It's the ongoing cause of Saint Margot, the modern saint who whips and torments people for their own good."

"Supposing she does," said Clara, "it's because she's frightened to death, right?"

"No, I don't think she's afraid. She's too proud. She's got her love of principle, provided it's bound to cause another pain. Even as a victim she could only succeed. Margot wants to be remembered by people—while they're writhing in the remorse she's tricked them into feeling."

"I doubt that very firmly," said Clara. "It sounds like your reading of Margot, and it's as crazy as any myth of hers. She's always behaved like a perfectly reasonable being with us—at times remote, certainly—but not fantastic and not cruel either."

"Sure, but she never stole anything from you, did she?"

"Not that I'm aware of."

"There, you see." Robert was quiet and put away his pipe. "It began again last night, even though she's not around. There's always a moment while I'm working, when I kick over into a sort of bliss. It's love for something beautiful from the past (allow me this), poised against all the music of the past. And suddenly everything's defiled because a vile image rises up from our experience—something she's had to tell me."

"Wait a minute," Clara said. "If these images come from your experience together, they could just be images you've put in her mind."

Robert looked interested.

"Maybe you've forgotten they're things she's heard you say. And if she says them back, it's so you'll grasp that someone's—she's—sharing your life; she doesn't know you said them only to expel them."

"Wonderful," said Robert, "except she has no idea of what I want and need."

"What you were just saying," said Patrice, "about images that interrupt your ecstasy reminds me that our other guest should be here at any minute."

Clara laughed out loud.

Patrice said, "I don't think either of you is behaving very sanely."

"You're right," said Robert. "Well, where is this guest, this victim of yours?"

Clara was not amused. "Honestly, Robert, stop calling people victims. He's a good fellow with a lot of nerve. You might even like each other. He's walking across the hills, so it can be a while."

"Of course it can—ah, the American abroad. Any amount of time squandered, any pointlessness, in the name of 'experience.'" And with a heavy accent, in a rich baritone: "Springtoime-in-Parris . . . ."

"I think you must be off your feed," said Clara. She sounded disappointed. "Maybe you should go home, and we'll see you soon on our own."

"No go, Clara. Not without supper. All right, I'm sorry. It's not your fault, and it probably isn't even the tenant's. It's Margot who does it to me every time, and you know that by now. Believe it or not, I'm overjoyed to see you, so don't make me go." He reached over and took her hand. "I saw something very odd last night on the road to Grasse—a hoot owl with a lizard in his beak." And he must have imitated the bird, because they all laughed.

Paul felt a sort of crazy joy to learn so much about Margot at once and so predictably from her appointed source, even if what he heard made her sound still more dangerous. He pulled back and leant against the side of the shed. He'd had enough of their conversation. He did not want to know what Robert had seen on the road to Grasse but rather everything that Robert knew about Margot and indeed what Robert "fantasized."

She wanted him to know what Robert knew; she wanted him to know the content of her myths. Strange, then, that she had written to everyone else about his arrival except Robert.

Paul worked his way quietly back to the path; then, putting the rucksack back on, he marched with a heavy tread toward the house. As he came closer to the group under the trees, he waved and shouted a greeting.

Clara got up smiling and walked toward him, meeting him halfway. He hugged her, and she stayed for a moment in his arms, responding to his warmth.

"I'm glad to see you," she said. "You know, I missed you after you went away last time. We had a good talk."

"Yes, we did. I'm very happy to be back again. Thank you for not having made me feel like an intruder. I don't know what I was thinking of when I came without phoning ahead."

"Never mind. Come on," she said, "I want you to meet Coustrieu." She took him by the arm and pulled him toward the others.

Robert shook his hand with little warmth and without a show of interest. Paul was relieved, realizing that he had been more afraid of Robert's studying and knowing him. Paul was free of his worry about anything that Margot might have told Robert, but Catherine could have said something to Robert that would have given him away. The danger wasn't great, however, that she could have said much more than that her lover for a night was occupying Margot's house and was also called Robert. And though Coustrieu had been quiet, he didn't seem puzzled when he heard that the tenant's name was Paul. It was even more interesting how effectively Catherine had concealed every trace of recognition of Margot's house. After all, even if Catherine had not been Margot's bondswoman for a night (and Paul had by and large rejected this thesis), she and Margot would surely have known each other. It was unlikely that Robert had never brought her to La Casaubade. Everything pointed to Catherine's exquisite discretion.

Robert looked at him over the rim of his wine glass as Paul shrugged off the knapsack and settled. "I hear you're living at Margot's. It means your landlady's in some other country where she's happier."

Paul felt torn in his loyalties. He wasn't ready to take in at such close range Robert's nastiness to Margot. That wasn't going to make his task of becoming Robert's confidant any easier. But Clara and Patrice almost in unison changed the subject, Clara looking at Robert very emphatically, so the mood grew safe. Patrice and Robert began ruing together the taxation of civilized pleasure, including the pleasure of tipping, under Mitterand. Paul found himself liking Robert. He could understand some of Robert's nervous outrage at Margot, however unexpectedly harsh; Paul knew in his bones she was a breeder of discord that went beyond saying or doing hurtful things. Her mere presence, actual or only hinted at, could bring about an intensification. She charged the rooms at La Casaubade, as here she charged the air. It had made him willy nilly eject Catherine from the place.

Robert turned to him. "You look absolutely exhausted, *Monsieur le prof.* Have some wine. That's a strenuous walk, isn't it?" His gaze wasn't friendly but neither was it unkind. He laughed. "Honestly, as much as I hate to speak this way, you Americans are all the same!"

"What?"

"You like to test yourselves, don't you? You're not sure you're all there unless you're going to some sort of extreme."

"That's our national habit—or predicament. We think we have to invent a new self everyday, and that self doesn't feel new unless it takes yesterday's a little further."

"Nonsense," said Robert. "You confuse experience with pathos. In America there's a neurosis in the air which the inhabitants mistake for energy." He laughed. "Guess whose line."

The company was silent.

"This fellow's landlady!" he snorted.

Paul was quiet. Robert or Margot had stolen the line.

"All right," said Robert, "who's for a game of *boules*? Patrice? Clara?"

"Not today," said Clara. "I couldn't stand the stress. Robert is a ferocious competitor," she said to Paul, "and that's putting it mildly."

Robert grinned. "Come on, Clara. Play."

"I can't. I have to prepare dinner."

"Patrice?"

"I'll play with you." He was smiling. "Watch out, I feel dangerous today." He rubbed his hands. "How about you, Paul? Do you want to join us?"

Robert turned and looked quizzically at him.

Paul smiled, relishing the moment. He could decline without shame, since the invitation was not serious. But he felt the thrill of pitting himself against Robert in a game at which he was by no means inept. He had played *bocci* during his summer in Florence. He had lived on the outskirts of town, on the road to Siena, and evenings would go down to the little square to watch the games. In the beginning the locals had paid no attention to him, but as they began to note his interest and fidelity they warmed to him, and one old man in particular had taken him on as a disciple. If not a prize pupil, he had become a worthy opponent. "I think I'll give it a try," he said.

Robert stared at him. "You know how to play?"

"I've played *bocci*. The games aren't that different, are they?"

"We'll hope for the best," said Clara, on a note of glee.

Patrice returned carrying the heavy silver balls, the dummy—hard, white, a sort of rubber golfball—and two twiglike measuring sticks. He drew lines with his heel. Robert, his pipe clenched between his teeth, a look of complete absorption on his face, rolled a silver ball smoothly and precisely across the field. His form was studied, the performance concentrated, from the steady aim-taking to the adroit snapping of the wrist. Between throws, the two of them—Robert and Patrice—kept up amiable chatter, full of exaggerated courtesy and then raw teases ("You keep rolling it too short!" "Too much spin, *mon vieux*!" "Oh, don't just sideswipe him"), lamenting the irregularities in the ground—Robert kept smoothing out the field with the side of his shoe—and admiring each other's play. Robert praised Patrice's tosses from where, with his hanger, he drew little crow's feet between the thrown and the stationary balls, a charade which, thought Paul, suitably masked Robert's pleasure in blasting his opponents off the court. Patrice behaved gallantly, yet with a certain irony, as if it were by agreement between them to allow Robert his little ruse of amiability.

As Patrice stood ready to aim, Paul whispered to Clara, who was watching on her chair, drinking wine and smoking, "Who usually wins?"

"I don't keep track, I'm not competitive. It's not that kind of game for me. It belongs to this country: I like the thumping of the balls on the dirt at the end of the day, a nice music for the dinner chores."

"More than just music. Look at Robert taking aim."

The tall figure stood upright, immobile for a moment, lustrous in a pool of shadow. Knees bent, he brought his arm back, wrist curved down, readying for a crucial throw. But just as his wrist was moving for release, Clara cried out in pleasure: an enormous radiant gypsy moth had settled on Robert's shoulder. Robert stopped, his exasperation barely concealed by an inquiring look. "Everything all right?"

"I'm sorry, Robert."

Robert looked at Paul, saying, "I thought he might have got you to distract me."

"That's unworthy of you," said Clara. "Come on, Robert, get on with it."

They did get on with it—with quiet intensity, aiming, pacing back and forth to see and measure and judge, calling out the score, calling exhortations. Robert had an edge on the others, but that seemed less the result of demonstrated skill than determination. They were at the point where three—or, if necessary, four—games would decide the outcome. The light was fading, their chatter had died away, the one sound was the clicking and thumping of the balls.

As soon as Robert won the first game, Paul knew that he did not want him to win the match, even if only Patrice stood to benefit. The next game was his own, on sheer adrenalin, and

Patrice won the third with what seemed an easy, careless throw. They were at the final game. Robert and Patrice had rolled well, each putting his ball within a few inches of the mark—Patrice's in front and Robert's to the side, somewhat closer. As Patrice's ball blocked the direct line to the mark, Paul had only one choice: he had to aim between it and Robert's, hoping to send Robert's spinning off, but there was little hope that his own would not follow after Robert's. If, on the other hand, he could put enough spin on the ball while hitting Robert's head-on, his own might stop close enough to the stake to win. He remembered how his old mentor had tried to teach him this throw, objecting that his hand was too stiff and his wrist not flexible enough, but after some weeks he had caught on and he too could execute the deadman's draw. That was years ago.

Now he stood, as serious as his opponent, feet to the line, eyes intent on the balls in front of him. Straightening up, he paced off ten strides to the rear; then, his forearm drawn back, he ran back up to the line and with a swift jerk hurled the ball bouncing and spinning across the field. It smacked Robert's ball off into the shadows as it itself dribbled to a halt, just outside the radius of victory already drawn by Patrice's.

There was a dead still moment.

"Well, thank you, old man," said Patrice. "A very nice shot. For me, that is." He smiled.

"A hell of a shot, I'd say." Robert looked back up at Paul, one eyebrow cocked, as he busied himself with the balls, in order, Paul was certain, as he watched him, to mask the force of his disappointment or indeed his fury. "At least we kept the win this side of the Atlantic."

It barely touched Paul's elation.

Robert dropped the balls into their box and then stood up, with a wild look, flinging an arm around Patrice's shoulder, crying, "Clara, some wine; a toast to your husband the victor— and I don't mean your barnyard white, I don't drink nail polish. Where's that Rausan-Segla you've been squirreling away?" He slapped his hands together. "Then we're onto serious things: your *poussins*—and my poison!" He laughed, settling himself briefly on the arm of the chair beside Clara. "I hear those thugs who smashed up the café got to Varda too. I'm sorry about that. As much as I think that old rat's nest wants clearing out"—he held up his hands, as if pleading with Patrice for agreement—"too many memorabilia of the good life, too self-consciously positive—still, I hear, it was hard on old Nick. Jaw to jaw with the knife-carrying, stinking-of-piss, anarchism-spouting riffraff of the Western world—no, not smart, not civilized. I admit, there's my bad side: I'd have liked to sit on the sidelines and witness his outrage. 'How dare you vandals assault our hard-won civility and good taste!' That's the trouble with types who worship civility, they can't stand being reminded of what it is that needs all the civilizing—the plain hatefulness of old Adam."

"He shot one of them in the leg," said Paul, "so perhaps he's more resourceful than you give him credit for."

Robert stared at him. "More power to him. I won't ask what he was thinking about when he did it. I'm always glad to hear that I've misjudged people. But what about you, *Monsieur flambeur-des-boules*, have I misjudged you?"

"You mean would I stoop to violence? I haven't killed anyone yet."

"No," said Clara, "Paul's still in the early stages. He still has to learn to cut up people with his tongue and spit them out and never even worry if it hurts." She touched Paul's shoulder and urged them all toward the house, distributing tasks with promises of rewards.

The meal was surprisingly easy. Robert—and Paul too—took over with jokes and fabulations, Paul growing less and less wary, Robert now not seeming to think of him as a spoiler or intruder and having evidently dropped (or put between brackets) the spy hypothesis. Then, immediately after coffee, Clara and Patrice begged weariness and early chores and went to bed, inviting their guests to help themselves to marc and mirabelle and make themselves at home.

They sat quietly. When the house had grown still, Robert tapped out his pipe and said, "Well, old man, what is it you want from me?"

Paul stared at him.

"Now, you do want something, don't you?" His tone was detached. "Come on. Those two have never asked me up here before. Sometimes I come of my own accord, or we run into each other, but we're not social animals. There's got to be some explanation for this novelty, and the only answer I can see is you."

Paul had not imagined such directness. "I'm sure I said I'd be interested in meeting you. You do get spoken about, you know—respectfully." He fingered the fraying cord on the armchair in which he was forced to slump too low, not unconfident, not wanting to be elsewhere, and yet not quite sure how to conduct his business.

"I know." Robert tossed his head impatiently. "I get served up with drinks by the expatriates of Seillans, who'll sell themselves to paint a look of interest on the blank faces of their neighbors."

Paul thought of Nicholas and Jean. "That's saying too much, unkindly."

"Have I attacked some of your friends? Oh, pardon, Monsieur."

"No, you're just being rude to your friends, and you choose the wrong target—the expatriate."

"You fail to notice that I'm including you in my attack. You also ignore my request, my very frank request, to tell me why you and I now find ourselves in the same room. I don't like chance in my life—outside of my music." He hesitated for a moment, then began to relight his pipe. "Take note, my friend, that I'm about to leave. It will be almost impossible for you to get your hands on me again, and then your motives will cease to matter. But I am curious, I grant you—not so much about you, of course: I suspect Margot is at work here and you're her tool. What's going on?"

"Why do you think she has anything to do with this meeting? I don't even know the woman. I only rent her house."

"So you don't know her from England or the States or wherever? Never mind. I don't need you to tell me where she lives." He was silent. "So she's only let you rent her house. She's given you tenure at La Casaubade, but you're utterly incurious about her."

Paul smiled. "I wouldn't say that. Of course one's curious about the person in whose house one lives."

Robert shook his head. "This defies credulity. Just tell it straight, will you?" He stood up, then turned and stared at Paul, pointing his pipe at him with small, impatient jabs.

"OK, I admit to arranging our meeting. You're supposed to be strong, so you can't be disturbed by a single, unprepared encounter, can you?"

Robert frowned.

"Or is that why you live alone? Because you can't give others what they want?" Paul was surprised at his own tone.

Robert raised his eyebrows, then looked as if he had decided to like this. He sat down. "That's better. You can be a bit rough. Though understand one thing: your criticism, as the criticism of a perfect stranger, leaves me ice cold. I've heard it all before, including the all-purpose insult narcissism."

"Look, I've heard about you," said Paul, "I repeat, always with respect—from a number of sources, whether you like it or not. I still don't understand why it's so important for you not to be spoken of. I've come here to live alone too, to try out my solitude. I'm interested in you as someone who seems to have suffered even more than I for the same good cause." Saying this, Paul felt miserable.

Robert studied him. "I'll tell you something. You can express an interest in solitude all you want, and make lists. You can arrange it while you're looking around for good examples and for people to talk about it with, but then your solitude is only a bait. If that's what you're doing, then you're not alone, and you never have been. You don't know what solitude is because all you've ever done is tell it, no doubt with great pride. But that's just vanity, because, Christ, you're like all those people who fall in love for the sake of a diary entry; you're solitary just long enough to tell the story."

Paul shrugged. "You sound just as self-conscious about it as you say I am. What's the point? Solitude's only for the happy few, in terrible isolation? Solitude's authentic when you're turreted away in a medieval house—in a jewel of a village—a tourist spot, no less? But what has that got to do with the rigorous, the compulsory solitude of the exiled?"

Robert snorted. "The expatriated."

"No," said Paul, "exile isn't voluntary."

Robert was on the verge of getting up. "What do you

know about exile? You're a professor on sabbatical. Listen, even in houses with turrets and views, Europeans live solitary lives. The fact that Americans find their houses picturesque has nothing to do with the quality of their solitude." He stopped, then said more quietly. "The way I live has nothing to do with elitism of any sort, that would be a plain contradiction in terms. If I believed in an elite, I'd be out more, looking for it. I just refuse to trivialize a hard and frightening life for the sake of conversation."

"Why is solitude so frightening?"

Robert half-turned away. He shook his head, then returned. "Because it's impossible to master, because it's so intense and empty." He paused. "Because it can be disgraceful, but you're stuck with it, you *are* it. I might be going on constructively or at least patiently for days—then all of a sudden, without warning, it's loose, twisting me away from myself, and then I—or it!—can only lurch about, out of control, and shake and tear at its invisible chains. Sometimes the slightest memory sets it off—an island off Mexico, a view in Umbria, a concert in Assisi almost heard." He stopped abruptly, then continued: "Moments one thought one had got over long ago.

"Other times it's a mood—of my death—yours is coming too, you know. It takes away all purpose. Ah, the stabs of anxiety—but in a way, they're crucial; they spur the search for form again." Robert was quiet now, perhaps from the effort of talking so much.

"One can get so damned furious and resentful about being alone. One wants the liveliness of another. I wanted it once, I don't anymore. It could have been a decent sort of dignity, an epicurean compromise. A woman who lived in Paris was going to come down here for part of the year. But all of a sudden that wouldn't work."

"She wanted something more definite?"

He shook his head. "No, something more definite would have been easier to deal with. She didn't want any such thing because we were of one mind about keeping our independence." Robert puffed his pipe toward the ceiling. "We were on the verge of that famous, that lovely unspoken harmony of intent, when she changed. She'd met someone and was being influenced. She wanted more of everything. She lost her delica-

cy and her sense of justice. Now there were nothing but con-
flicts and demands—willfulness."

"What was changing her?"

"Don't be obtuse. You must have gathered by now that it
was Margot."

Paul was aroused. "But why? Because she wanted you for
herself?"

Robert looked almost hurt. "Are you a fool? She wanted
her for herself."

Paul struggled to keep Robert talking. "You must have
known Margot very well."

"Yes," said Robert, "We know each other very well. You
might say I know her story."

"She's told you her life story?"

"Yes," said Robert, "most of it, in the course of the years."

"I write to her," Paul said. "I confide in her, I think it's in
response to her confidential tone, but I still don't know her.
Perhaps she doesn't want to be known."

Robert was silent.

"Perhaps she just doesn't like people very much."

"Margot hates in individual cases, too."

"Yes, I know. Even though you withdraw, you need to
keep close to you just a little of something you despise in order
to justify yourself. God forbid that a self-imposed exile, maintained over years of sacrifice, should be ruined by the hint that
there'd been something better to do. But look at this house:
how could you or she just ignore Patrice and Clara? They'd
shake anybody's resolution and any misanthropy, I think."

"No they wouldn't: they're fine, but don't forget they live
under a protective illusion."

"Which is?"

"The illusion of romance." Robert made a gently dismis-
sive gesture.

"What about Nicholas and Jean? They share a life."

"You know what's going on there as well as I. It's the
stable relation of unequals. Jean surrenders by giving Nicholas
the illusion that he's always inventing things. Meanwhile, he
shuts up about his boredom and Nicholas' repeating himself,
because Jean thinks he could't do any better."

"They quarrel. I've seen Jean arguing with Nick."

"Yes, fighting and making up: that's the cultural excitement of the petite bourgeoisie."

"Petite bourgeoisie—Varda and Jean Abels?"

"Oh let's not quibble. 'Petit bourgeois' is an attitude."

"Well," said Paul, "you see easily enough what compromises the others, so what about your own case? What was so threatening to you and Margot?"

"Nothing." Robert looked at him.

"I meant, before Catherine."

Robert leapt up. His face was white. "What the . . . !" He stared at Paul. "How the hell did you know her name?" He clenched his fists. "Fuck you gossiping idiots. Look at you—so civilized, so articulate—hungry for details, hungry for another man's life. Haven't you got a life of your own? You don't want to borrow mine, I can tell you, and, anyway, it's mine—got it? I put it together for my use, not yours."

Paul tried to object.

"Quiet!" Robert roared. "Go feed somewhere else. I hate your bloody prying. How much do you know already anyway? How long have you been running around here asking questions in that anthropological way of yours? I'll bet you've found one informant after another—full of choice news and if it's malicious, all the better. That's when they're not getting drunk on it themselves, wasps buzzing in a bottle, sucking up the sorrow of other peoples' lives!" And without another word, Robert raged out of the house, and within seconds, Paul heard the groaning of the engine as he drove his car away in first gear.

The silence descended on him. He sat empty, outraged, unable to move, unable to think. The name Catherine could do such damage.

Chapter Ten

M y dear Paul,

So at last you've met Robert, and I see you've been captured by his arrogant charm. It's strange on the face of it how these qualities can be associated. It must be that arrogance, more than any other sort of pretension, only reveals the fragility it's supposed to hide, reveals it to us but leaves its bearer lost and duped—yet touching.

As I reread your lines, I'm brought back into your midst. Your description of Robert, however, is richer than your news. I'm certain he had a good deal to say, but you're really quite reticent on this point. Paul, could you be a little more forthcoming in the future? You must, of course, if we are to have the success we are working so hard to achieve.

I was disturbed that your meeting ended badly. It is a great waste, although I can understand your wanting to provoke him. But you know as well as I that driving him back into his cave is wrong. Your bond with Robert is too important to let vanity come between you. Please make every effort to right this situation. There is no way your life at La Casaubade is going to flourish without him. You will fall back into the "simple bliss" of all the others there.

Remember, you wrote that you were willing to risk everything, to confront on equal terms the *démon du Midi*. Don't
throw away the chance before you've taken it. You must go to
the very root of your being if you want what La Casaubade can
give you. It is something that lies beyond civility. You must train
every instinct to endure a kind of violence, even to the point of
being overcome. Paul, do you understand? Only then, when
you cannot bear it any longer, turn away but not before: you will
have risked everything, and that single excitement will justify
your life.

Robert knows. He knows it better now that Catherine's
gone, who was his alibi against the real living life. It doesn't
matter that he misses her: these feelings will only strengthen
him. You were right to curb your impulse to know her. I shall
say nothing more about this.

It's the end of fall now, and the colors in the Var will have
deepened, not to the burst red and gold of New England, but to
a softer shade, as though the land had begun the journey back
into itself. In your hills it is time for withdrawal, for ingathering
and retirement. Everywhere else the coming of winter brings
people together: they gather to eat game, drink wine, talk, comfort one another; but where you are, like things in nature, you
withdraw into yourself to gather force before the sun burns
again at the zenith.

This time of year in France, I usually give up social life. My
mood is partial to cloisters, dens, and ruins. In winter I return to
a place closer to the earth from which I can see but not be seen;
there I contemplate the power of the seasons and the barren
follies of my kind. The riches of the first are not so evident as in
summer, against the depth of green, but they are present in the
changing line of hills, the fine mutations of brown and gray, the
sudden crash and dart of creatures, the swooping of a falcon
overhead. The sun no longer burns, but now that it no longer
dazzles, it reveals. Sit under the chestnut tree, and the winter
light will show you things you've never seen.

In winter Robert becomes a reader again and feeds on the
latest theoretical imports from Paris. He spends his afternoons
at a little bookstore in Draguignan called Lo Pais. There, where
he is known only as a customer, he often lets the afternoon slip
away, browsing and talking with the gentle fellow who runs the
shop. Sometimes the two of them go off and have a beer if
Robert is around at closing time.

Try again with him; believe me, you cannot complete your

adventure on your own. You need him now to give directions, to heighten its intensity. You should arrange to run into Robert at the bookstore; this time come better prepared. Engage him, interest him, make no allusion to your last meeting. Take the chance and capture him. Make the meeting short and without complaint—I'll help you with the next.

Has he spoken of me to you?

Be vigilant.

Margot

Paul had found the letter after returning from Seillans, where he'd been caught in a rainstorm. Half-undressed, water running down his face and dripping onto the sheets, he read it at the kitchen table. The rain had stopped, and now the hills were engulfed in gray, swirling, soaking fog. There was nothing outside, except gray billows pierced by the spiny branches of the olives.

As Paul returned to the letter, he started; a face was at the glass door—Jules. Paul let him in. The kitchen filled with the smell of sour wine, damp oilskin, and wet dog. Paul shoved his papers aside for him to sit down at the table; he went to warm up the coffee and poured marc into the steaming mugs. Jules offered him a Gauloise; the harsh draw of smoke against his throat felt good.

"So," said Paul, "what brings you up here in weather like this? I'm glad you came. I was thinking it was the end of the world."

"*Ben, M'sieur.*" Jules nodded. "It's never that bad. There are always one or two things to give good comfort—and me, I'll take the bottle. Good cheer there is in a bottle and always the same. Maybe in a good woman, too, but good ones aren't easy to find, not around here anyway with me getting older and more choosy." He smiled through his three teeth.

Paul looked at him.

"You know what it's like. Let a female in, and before you know, she'll do everything her way and drive you madder than any old fog, mark me."

"I can't live with a woman whom I don't like enough or with one I like too much."

Jules said, "You can't live on your own." He poured more

marc into the mug and peered at Paul. "*Ben, M'sieur*, how are you faring? Not looking as good as you did. You're too young to give up women. Time enough for that when your chin has bristles and your joints are stiff."

Paul nodded.

"Don't talk about peace, that's what she used to do; it's all excuses. She was longing for a man—all that pacing up and down like a vixen in a cage. Don't want to see you like that, it's a waste. There are nice young things in the village. If I was a bit younger and quicker afoot, I'd be chasing them myself, but now understanding is all I've got left. So you do as I say."

"You're probably right."

Jules smiled. "It's many years I've been watching the goings on of men and women, and you foreigners are no different. You want to go off on the chase, but first take that sad look off your face. It's winter, but there's still life going on, more than ever now the harvest's over. You mark me."

"I do mark you, Jules. I just haven't felt much like chasing women. This year is different. I've come here to be on my own—to think and do my work."

"Ah, your work? You've done a lot, have you?" Jules looked at him, over the rim of the cup, eyebrows raised.

"You stab me there. No."

"Well, you see. It isn't natural. What do folks like you and she want to come here for, all alone, away from where you belong, away from what you're supposed to be doing?"

"And what is that? What am I supposed to be doing?"

"You should be raising your children and thinking about what you're going to leave behind. Me, I think of these things, but it's not easy. All I can leave behind is some olive trees and some earth I've worked, but that is something for those who come after me."

Paul nodded and lit a Gauloise.

"Not, mind you, that my children care. They've gone down to the coast to work for the foreigners. All they think about is motorcycles and loud music. A great shame it is: they should be trying to educate themselves for a better life. But you can't talk sense to them. My father always wanted me to learn a trade, but I wouldn't listen. But I like the earth and my own little bit of it." For a moment the old man was quiet, looking into the bottom of his cup, his lips pursed. "They found a dead woman on the upper *berge* yesterday. Her body was fairly gone."

"Who was it? Where?"

"Not all that far from here. Up the road behind the house at the bottom of the clearing."

"Who was it?"

"I don't know. Nobody knows for sure."

"Who did it?" And Paul knew the thugs had done it. Oh my God, the pit bull had bitten her face off. He was the next target. They'd been at the house.

"*Ça travaille dans ma tête.* I had a letter from Madame yesterday. Needed a bit of help reading it, but Antoine at the café read it to me, he's quiet, doesn't go about blabbing. Madame wanted me to write her whether you were having any visitors."

Paul felt the irritation shoot up in him. "So she wants you to spy on me?"

"A while back, when I came up to the house in the morning, I looked in. You were gone, but there were people in the kitchen, drinking coffee and talking. They stayed a while, then left."

"Yes," said Paul, "friends of mine. But of course, you'll recognize . . . ." And then he bit his tongue; he wasn't about to help Jules tell Margot that he had slept with Catherine. "Never mind." And who the devil knew who'd been dug out of the *berge*. He wanted to go right to the police to find out but remembered angrily he still hadn't applied for a residence permit. To judge from the modus operandi of the law around here, the remotest accessory was at once considered a target of pursuit.

Jules was staring at him. Paul said, "So did you write to Madame Stevens about my friends?"

"I didn't think I should tell Madame that. I told Antoine— he wrote back for me—saying you were a good tenant and there were no guests and you looked after the property and the house looked like it always did."

Paul bit his lips. He had been right from the beginning, she was having him spied on from all sides. He had to force himself to swallow the coffee. "You did the correct thing, Jules. Thank you for telling me." He reached into his trousers and found a fifty franc note, which he handed over. Jules nodded.

By now the fog had cleared a little, and the shapes of the rosemary hedges were emerging outside the window. The dog Tintin was standing at the door begging to go out; Jules started to pull on his clothes and pack away his cigarettes.

"You're not going to work now, the ground is far too wet."

"No, no, the worms'll do the digging for me now, but I better be getting home before the storm."

Paul thought of the salvaged corpse. "Is it going to start again?"

"It always does around here. If you have one, then you're in for a few. Now remember what I said. Don't stay stuck away in this house all alone. It's not good for you or anyone. Didn't do her much good, did it?"

"*Who?*"

"Madame, of course." The old fellow grinned at him and ambled out, whistling for the dog. "See you in a couple of days, M'sieur."

Left alone, Paul sat still, clenching his jaw, able at last to have a single strong emotion. Damn! How dare she pursue him so blatantly, setting up the others with innocent-sounding letters, involving even Jules. For all he knew she might be here herself, commuting from Paris, peering from time to time through the kitchen window. What did she know, what was she finding out? Had she also been poking into American sources? He got up. Perhaps she was preparing to have him killed. No, it wasn't possible.

His eyes fell on the table and the letter. He gripped the back of the chair, staring with disgust at her letter as though it were alive. She was making his life dangerous. He marched out onto the terrace and stalked up and down on the gravel.

The letter was a provocation—dangerous for Margot and for him. She was on the verge of losing him: the tone was exalted and unbelievable, and it was peremptory; she was manipulating him. But whatever he felt didn't matter—he was lost either way. If he didn't do what she wanted, he would reproach himself afterward for everything he'd missed. If he did act, he was moving further toward suicidal entanglement. The thought frightened him and excited him. He could feel her urging him into a physical space, making him believe in the inevitability of his being there with her—so as to comfort her.

Why had he thought that? Comfort her? She was strong

enough as it was. Her letters asserted her strength and went on imposing it. But why him? Strong or weak, he thought, she wouldn't lose him. She'd been very clever: in choosing him she'd chosen well. He knew this. She would have had a number of plausible responses to the ad. But what in his letter had made him seem so pliable? Never mind, he'd had to go abroad, and it was inevitable that he be in France. He was right to have let himself be so used. He regretted nothing.

It was getting cold and dark. He went back in and sat down, his cheek propped up on his fist. He was drinking marc. The only sound was the drip from the gutter above the kitchen door. He wanted to escape from Margot's watchful eye.

As he sat—tired, wishing for another's voice—he heard a sound overlapping the rain dripping through the gutter. He listened to this small but persistent thumping, scraping, stony sound: it was as if he had heard it before, but when? Perhaps he had heard it in his sleep. He got up, puzzled. It stopped. He went back to the table. There was only the stowed-up rainwater, and then the sound came again, as if some live thing were stuck in the stone and were sawing its way out.

The *loir*? the dormouse?

Its turds were everywhere, it gnawed the bananas. He had resented it for weeks.

His companion—a mouse—and now this creature was loose and strident, impudent spirit of filth and lies and flies! The queer chordal sound stopped, then began again. He listened. He wanted to go on hearing it. For a while it seemed less sinister than before, almost likeable, like the rhythmic scraping of a child's toy.

He tried to locate it. It was hard to know whether it came from inside or outside the walls. If outside it could just be Jules's cat, Titi. Paul hurried to the French doors and peered out. At first he saw nothing; then, indeed, he saw the fat cat sitting on the ledge, licking its paw in the lowering light.

He turned back. The scraping went on. It was coming from the sofa, with its piled rugs. But since it was the dormouse, the cat could catch it. He flung open the door and ran outside, swooped down on the comatose creature, and lugged it into the room. The sound continued, but the cat seemed uninterested.

He ran into the kitchen, pulled open the utensils drawer,

and took out the carving fork. He raced back to the sofa and with his left hand grabbing firmly the pile of rugs, yanked them from the couch. Nothing.

What then?

The tapestry! The Albigensian zodiac was harboring the vermin.

He pulled up the tapestry. And there it was, right there, a furry gray muscled blob on the raw stone. His heart was racing. He lunged—here, there, here—stabbing with the metal and missing, stupidly bending the tines against the stone.

Suddenly the dormouse shot laterally across the wall and shimmied onto the upper wooden frame of the tapestry. Paul got up on the chair and tried to plunge at the rod but to his dismay pierced the topmost edge of the tapestry. The mouse clambered straight up the wall and settled at a spot just under the ceiling. Paul muttered that he now knew what the exposed stones were good for. He gazed up at the creature out of range, then ran into the kitchen and fetched sponges, which he began hurling up at the ceiling. You throw in the sponge!

But if the sponges were without effect, not so their flying shadows, which urged the creature along the edge of the wall and, Paul saw, within range of the upstairs balcony. He grabbed the fork and raced upstairs and leaning over the railing found the mouse within easy reach. The look of a trapped soul. Like a flash his fork flicked out and hit. Exultantly he watched it drop dead, down onto the sofa; then he rushed downstairs for his trophy. For a moment the mouse seemed to have disappeared into the pillows, but then there it was in plain sight.

Paul lightly poked its belly—and in a flash the creature twisted onto its legs and scuttled under the sofa. It had only been playing dead!

Paul dove down under the skirt of the sofa and eyed it huddled in its corner. He placed the prongs of his fork against its chest and with sick unhappiness, muttering, "Sorry, sorry," dug them in.

The dormouse twisted onto its back, shuddered, its rear leg twitched, it was finished.

Paul's heart was pounding, his whole body trembled. He took the corpse by the tail and brought it outside, showing it to Titi, who was crouching in astonishment. The cat watched him, barely sniffed, and sprang away.

Paul flung the creature over the *berges*. A wave of happy excitement spread through him. He lay back on the sofa, then swiftly dialed a number.

"Hullo, Robert?"

"What?"

"It's Paul. Paul van Pein."

The other's voice was silent.

"You remember me. Margot's tenant."

"Where the hell did you get my number from? It's unlisted."

"Margot left me a list of important phone numbers."

"I hate to be phoned."

"Oh, I'm sorry."

"What is it?"

"I wanted to tell you—I hope you don't think this is too strange—I've killed. I've killed a dormouse. I stabbed it, and I've had the wildest sense of exhilaration . . . and horror! It's something I had to tell somebody who'd understand."

"You what?"

"I've killed this animal, a dormouse. The thing was vexing me, was an enemy, and alive. I've killed it. And I feel a sort of crazy horror and joy."

Robert was silent.

"You remember, at Clara and Patrice's, we were talking about how Americans need each day to invent, to perform a self. Well, this was no performance. This is the real thing. I've touched something primitive at the bottom of my being. I can kill. I've hit old Adam, violent at the core. I tell you if there is a self, then this is the knowledge it has to be built on."

Robert was silent.

"You understand me, don't you?"

He heard a crash on the other end of the wire.

"Eh, Robert?"

He had hung up.

Fuck it! Paul went into a rage, he couldn't say whether more at Robert's rudeness or at his own impulsiveness. Had he gone absolutely out of his mind? He's ruined things between them a second time, not to mention his own pure thrill.

He paced. What was sickening he blamed on Robert, who had been the first to speak of violence—of rebarbative old Adam. But that wasn't the right old Adam, either. There had been his first Adamic experience on the *berge*—of clairvoyance deeper than violence and shattered by the violent barking of a dog. Robert and Margot were the great ambassadors of violence around here. If Paul had resisted them better, he would not have been inclined to prove the point by spearing a mouse. Silly? But it's no light thing killing a mammal.

The matter, however, was more complex than that. Paul could not deny that killing the *loir* had produced a basic state of bliss, all tension assuaged, until talk had fouled it again. Robert's rudeness had been inexplicably hurtful. He felt lonely, futile, used up; he was beset by an image of the soft gray coat of the dead dormouse. It had an intelligent face: it was almost as if—a child—he had murdered a playmate. He was invaded by the certainty of retaliation by a gigantic *loir*.

He remembered from Kafka the desperate sentence, "In the next room they are speaking of vermin." The world comes in two parts: those who speak of vermin and those who turn themselves into vermin.

Enough! He would get out, it was time—he would go . . . to Paris. In Paris, there would be streets, cafés, friends. He sat up straight. Paris was Catherine. Her carnal memory ran over his inner sense; he felt excitment. She had never replied to the note he'd sent her. No doubt she was still furious, but it would make all the difference when he explained things in person. He would charm his way back.

He got on the phone and booked space on the night train and a room at the Hôtel Scandanavie. He realized he would have to call Catherine. His hand lingered on the warm receiver: he needed first to think up a couple of reasons why she'd be out and a couple of anodyne explanations. Finally, knowing that he had no choice but to call if he was not to spend the week standing outside her building or every museum and art gallery in Paris waiting for her to show up, he dialed her number and listened to it ring.

"Catherine?"

"Yes."

"This is . . . Robert." He remembered just in time.

There was a pause. "I'm sorry, I don't know you."

Embarrassed, he stammered, "We met in Seillans in September, and you wrote me a deservedly harsh note."

Silence. "Yes?"

What else had he expected? "I wonder if you ever received my letter."

"I may have. I don't remember."

"Aha," said Paul. "I'm leaving for Paris tonight and hoped you might allow me to explain my explanation. Can we meet tomorrow evening? I'd be most grateful."

"I can't imagine what you still have to say."

"Catherine, listen to me. I know I behaved abominably after our last meeting. You have every reason not to trust me, but no matter what you think, I haven't forgotten you for a moment, and I'd like to try to make amends."

"I suppose it can't do any harm. I'm having dinner with a friend tomorrow, but I could be free around 10:30. We could meet at Balzar's, it's near where I live."

"Yes, I know where you live," said Paul, and he told her how he had got her address from the mayor.

She laughed. "Still living novelistically, eh?"

"Starting now, yes—I mean, starting now, no," said Paul.

He leapt up the stairs, exultant that she had agreed to meet him; he could sail off with the firm knowledge that he was expected. He packed feverishly, urged on by the memory of the aborted trip to London. This time he would get away. An hour later, having grabbed a raincoat and collected his books and money, he was in the 4CV, spinning his wheels on the sharp left turn in front of Varda's. As he sped along the darkening road, he found himself, to his delight, shouting: "This, this, is exactly what I want!"

Chapter Eleven

An immaculate woman in a plum velvet dress was sitting alone in the dining car, studying the menu. As Paul approached, she put down the card, removed her round rimless glasses, and looking directly at him, smiled radiantly. She was nearly forty and rather heavily made-up like an actress on stage, her hair an extraordinary reddish-golden color. She turned to look out the window, and her low-cut dress exposed broad, well-tanned shoulders and the outline of her full breasts. She wore a gold salamander at the cleavage.

Paul stared at her. "Good evening," he said. "May I join you?"

She beckoned to him to sit down.

"May I order something for you?"

"I'm not hungry," she said. "I never eat railroad food."

"Neither do I," said Paul. "I only came in to break up the trip."

She smiled to acknowledge, Paul thought, a parallel asceticism, which was trenchant sensuality in another guise; or perhaps she had seen through his gallant companionable pretense—he was hungry and had come to eat.

Paul ordered a bottle of Pommery "Louise," which he invited the woman to share. She accepted, then alluded to a full and well-travelled past and to mysterious preoccupations. Paul took in the excitement of her personal beauty, the cold shock of

141

the wine, and the thrill of rapid movement as they raced into the night. Like a guest at an evening affair alert to the dress code, Paul summoned up and put on the personality of Robert, world-famous writer of books on Central European angst and government. "You would recognize my surname," he said, "but I'd rather not tell you."

"Don't feel obliged to tell me anything," she said, smiling. Her dimpled cheeks belied an air of moral strenuousness.

Paul was conjuring with his power to construct a story as allusive and glamorous as her own, and besides, he had help: he had only to nourish his fiction with the traits and experiences of Robert Coustrieu. This extravagant woman gave the impression of a perfect complicity, or so Paul concluded from her lingering at the table in a state of peaceful animation.

All of a sudden she interrupted him. "I'm tired," she said. "I want to go to bed now." With surprising speed she got up, slid out, and stood up. Paul could not stop his left hand from flying out, as if to hold her by the wrist. She took his hand and pressed it firmly. He sat back down at the table, staring out the window—seeing nothing, replaying her words and looks and movements. Although their exchange had ended abruptly, he was certain that they would find themselves together again in first-class compartments, luxurious *relais* and châteaux, three-star restaurants, and New Year's Eve balls. He staggered to his *wagon-lit* and slept excitedly.

When, jolted awake, he saw the compartment door slide open, he thought for a moment that it was she, coming to make love to him. It was a porter bringing him the breakfast tray he had not ordered, but there was an envelope beside the coffee pot. He tore it open. It said, "This evening—the Ritz Bar at six-thirty—Marguerite." He gave the porter a 100 franc note.

Outside the Gare de Lyon, more sordid than usual because of a cleaners' strike, Paul walked along a dank, grimy street and into an old-fashioned café with dirty string curtains, aspidistras, and gold lettering on the glass. The windows were steaming; a number of workers in cobalt blue overalls stood at the zinc bar, puffing Gauloises, downing small glasses of Sancerre, and talking loudly about the latest misdeeds of Them. With a sense of old pleasure—it was like slipping into a Courbet painting—Paul slid onto a cracked red leather bench, ordered rolls and coffee, lit a Gauloise, and, scanning a copy of *Libération*, lost himself in astonishment at the crudeness of the anti-American propaganda. He was not surprised to overhear from the bar remarks of the same stripe, spoken in a vehement barking tone well suited to the ignorance informing them. Certainly, Paul was already acquainted with the view that the entire executive branch of the United States was *une bande de cons*. But he had heard it chiefly from wealthy older types around New York, whose whole mental endowment seemed to consist in the refrain that nowadays everyone was an idiot. While perhaps not truly superior, these speakers were at least grown up—but the squad at the bar with screwdrivers behind their ears? Paul gulped his coffee and, unable to catch the attention of the waiter, went up to the cash register to pay. One of the workers, sensing his impatience, said to him, "This isn't McDonald's."

"It may come as a surprise to you," said Paul, "but I can tell a McDonald's from a propaganda mill." He waited for the bartender. "And another thing I recognize when I hear it is knee-jerk Stalinist nostalgia."

The workman, outraged, fired a shaft at Paul's cryptoimperialism. The others drew closer.

Paul wondered aloud if they'd thought out the anti-democratic implications of heavily-taxed West Texas crude.

"Fuck West Texas crude," replied the biggest one, who wore around his neck a kerchief that Paul had last seen in the Apthorp on a Labrador retriever. France was for the French, and more or less for Iraq; and America, for all he cared, could continue to stick its nose up Berlin's arse, a fat lot of good it would do her. His smaller buddy then chimed in to remind them of Washington's exploitation of the Micronesian labor market, while the first returned briefly to the role of the Red Army in having paved the way for the liberation of Alsace.

"Quiet down or leave," the owner suddenly said—to Paul!

But his adversaries intervened, seeming eager to keep him until he had been rehabilitated, whereupon the owner offered them marcs. Like Freemasons engaged in an esoteric rite of unification, they solemnly stirred the liquor into their coffee grounds and nodded.

Paul was euphoric after checking into the Hôtel Scandanavie, where he and Michael had stayed until Léon could be imposed upon. It would have been brash to go directly to the Hôtel Collège de France. His joy was heightened by the consciousness of his own discretion—part of a sense of vertical transformation, of his occupying a superior place in knowledge and mood. It was a change he could measure only by returning to the very place he'd once set out from.

He did his lotus positions in order to propitiate the good gods for his evening's apppointments. At least it satisfied him that he hadn't left anything undone that could possibly be of use. Then he walked through the Luxembourg Gardens, smiling into the sun, groaning with pleasure, on impulse chatting with a children's nurse from Martinique. Life was senseless, impossible—hence, a certain good would be to palliate the bitterest consciousness of this evil, and the most effective palliative was action. He saw an omen in the lucky conversations he'd struck up with others. It made him feel easy and secure; add Catherine's willingness and Marguerite's invitation, and he was invincible.

To celebrate good prospects, Paul headed for a luxurious restaurant off the rue de Rivoli, where he sat on a salmon-colored banquette, drinking tender Château Léoville and jotting down life-affirming reflections. Toward the end of lunch, he found himself converging on a group with a pronounced North African character. A party was sharing an opulent meal, the centerpiece of which was a fish the size of a Roman dolphin that had been treated like meat and roasted in brown juices. The two male hosts—sleekly tailored, clean-shaven, with bluish jowls—looked like aging polo players. Their wives had the profiles of empresses in Byzantine frescoes, with thick upswept hair and clusters of glittering jewels at their ears and necks. Their kohl-rimmed eyes bulged as bright as owls'. A plump woman turned toward his table—breathless and perfumed, every sigh enthusiastic. She handed him a glass of champagne flavored with kumquat syrup. "Do you always stare at people so intently?" she asked.

Paul lowered his gaze. "No."

"Oh, I didn't mean now," she laughed. "I meant before, when you were having lunch. That's why I'm speaking to you, because of your inquisitive eyes. Meet my cousins. This is Farah, and this is Sarnia."

Paul was once again Robert. The hostess left: her friends looked him over boldly. Their smiles were more affluent than their words, which were casual but not unkind, for they seemed to acknowledge his right to be among them. He heard the men muttering of arbitrage and stock indexes. The world was a vast Casbah of investment opportunities. The women were speaking among themselves. Paul got up and approached an exalted-looking European brunette in boots, sitting with the back of one thigh hitched up on a table.

"Oh look," she said, "someone as out of place as I. Come on, sit beside me." Her voice was accented and lilting.

Paul climbed up, smiling.

She put her cheek next to his. "I'm probably the only woman in the room who could tell you what these men really care about."

"Yes? And how do you come by such information?" She was tipsy. He leant close. He could smell her perfume like oleander and the powder that had softened her cheeks that morning.

She laughed. "That's obvious, isn't it? I belong to one of them, I'm a collectible. Don't pretend to be shocked: he's not old and fat—he's forty and good-looking, and he rides and flies and keeps falcons and is dull only because he's sure of me."

"So young and yet so price-conscious," said Paul, looking into her green wolf's eyes.

"When you've been raised in provincial Iceland and you dream of Paris, you'll pay a price for it. It begins with becoming a *fille au pair* in a snobby, ungrateful family, and then you pay a bigger price in order to stay, even though Paris is no longer the rush it once was."

She knew a life which Paul could only guess at. He was tickled to be her confidant.

"I understand," he said. Her smiles were trickling into him like drops of golden harquebusade into his belly. He had to stop himself from touching the line of her naked shoulder and upper arm so that that curve would be stored in his fingertips. He wanted to be able to lean against her whenever he liked;

now it was as if they were sitting on a swing, but the exhilaration was greater because of the headier medium they were swinging through—worldliness.

He reached for two glasses of champagne from a passing tray, gave her one, and said, "But there are compromises less drastic."

"None as clear-cut."

"And that's the point?"

"Listen, I do what I do in spite of what's right. Just like everyone else."

Paul objected.

"All right, like everyone of these women. I like having a man explain to me exactly what my choices are and then forcing me to make the right one." She laughed.

Paul said, "I believe you're quite serious."

"I am serious, that's true, but about other people's lives— not my own."

"I hope that's your mood now. Would you like to be serious about another man's life?"

She frowned abruptly. "I only meant I'm good at telling my friends who live like me that they've done the right thing." Paul watched her intently. "So, you'd like me to be serious about you if only for a little while?"

Yes, he crowed silently. "I'll take responsibility," he said.

She was thinking. "We would have to share the responsibility."

He nodded his head slowly, his eyes darting over her eyes, her neck, her shoulders. "Are you saying by any chance that you'll come away with me?"

"Let me see what I can do." An arm suddenly encircled her shoulder, and a dark, handsome face appeared beside her cheek. "Ready, Katja? It's time we went." The man did not acknowledge Paul.

She turned to Paul. "I have to go now."

Paul watched them walk toward the door. She put on a shiny black fur jacket; but then he saw her make excuses, and she was coming back to him. His heart jumped. "You see," she said, "this sharing responsibility—it's no good. Someone has to be in charge."

"I could be in charge," he whispered.

"No." She shook her head. "Impulses are just luxuries, anyway."

"Wait." He held her hand, his thumb barely touching the inside of her wrist. "I really need to see you."

She was savoring, perhaps, the moment of his folly. "I'm sure we'll meet again. I'll be at the Opera on Friday," and she sprang away.

It dawned on Paul that he could have been killed. And yet he felt full. He saw himself staying till Friday, until he conjured the boredom and dismay of waiting for her and her not actually turning up. And certain that she would not come, he felt the gold seep away, leaving him forlorn. He was furious at women.

"Katja's a regular heartbreaker," said his hostess, beside him; she had taken his hand and was leading him back to her friends. "A fatal combination: innocence and ennui. Masoud knows exactly when to rescue her."

She was wrong to think that Katja had needed to be rescued.

The woman laughed. "But she always lets herself be. Now, come on, don't look so solemn: have some champagne and tell me whom you're seeing in Paris."

Paul remembered with a start the answer to this question and darted a glance at his watch. There was still a little time, so he let himself be enveloped by her indifferent generosity. He settled among the women, excited by their flashing eyes and shining dresses. Each wore the same gold Rolex watch. Was this a harem? He felt that if he stayed any longer he would dissolve from the strangeness. It was already five. He got up: he would have to hurry to change and be at the Ritz on time.

He lay back on the heap of pillows, rotating a crystal snifter, waiting for Marguerite to return. They had made love excitedly, starting in the taxi when he had touched her knee. She had managed to slip down a little, the taxi had lurched, and his fingers had stroked her thigh under her skirt to discover, as he shuddered, that above the tops of her stockings she was naked.

She had given thought, he mused admiringly, to his seduction. She had waited for him in the bar, with only a hint of impatience at his tardiness, dressed in a strawberry-colored blouse which focused the wild gleams of strawberry blond in her hair, a silken mulberry-colored rose at her cleavage, and a violet wool skirt carefully draped around her long legs. And now in the paneled bedroom, full of silk and mauve velvet and soft wools, even the air was voluptuous and scented. A rosy cashmere blanket covered the foot of the bed. On the ottoman a silken rug spread out, trailing its fringes over the worn Tabriz beside the lion-claw feet of an old escritoire. Above it hung a gilt-framed oval mirror. Beside a double window covered with grey satin, an opaline bowl of gardenias gleamed, their dense scent drenching the warm air.

Marguerite stood in front of him in a loose kimono, her hair pulled back from her face, her cheeks flushed, her eyes glittering.

"I love this time of the night," she said, "when everything is quiet and secluded." Her perfect tones seemed practiced.

Suddenly the image of the harsh sun striking off purple hills affected Paul with an almost physical sensation of longing.

"Even as a child," said Marguerite, "I used to stay up all night. My brother and I would wake each other when everything was dark and quiet and the sounds of the streets had died away." She leaned back on the cushions of the velvet divan opposite the bed. "We'd go prowling. We had a cache of candles. We'd discover things. We'd drink Papa's special liqueurs and explore forbidden places—like his study, where he'd hidden away his illustrated books: *The Golden Ass, The Decameron, The Empire of the Senses*. Once we smoked his clove-scented cigarettes from Bali, but Eric had a coughing fit. I thought we'd be caught, so I stuffed the drapery into his mouth."

Paul stared at her.

"Later on we read Papa's correspondence. He had gambling debts—this we could make out—and there were letters which suggested that Maman was having an affair with his younger brother, a Navy chaplain stationed at Toulon."

"You were surprised?"

"We were shocked. But since we had always thought we were adopted, we treated these bits of news like intrigues in a novel. We tried to predict her comings and goings but did so only at night and never said anything to her during the day, when she teased or scolded us like thoughtless children. It was as if this adulterous woman had an only nocturnal existence because that was when we studied her."

Paul said, "I know what it's like to be a child-spy."

Marguerite smiled. "I think there's a good deal of likeness to our lives." She studied him for a moment. "My secret nights began to change. My brother went off to school. I carried on my watches, but they weren't the same."

"How so?"

"They were more intense, more fanciful—also sadder and lonelier. Gradually, I realized I didn't need Eric for the best night work." She smiled. "I read Baudelaire by candlelight and wrote poems like a tiger tearing meat. I wrote about mirrors that swallowed you up and rooms that disappeared. I couldn't wait for him to come home on holiday, so I could show him my discoveries. But he didn't want to be with me anymore; he thought our night games were child's play."

"And so," said Paul, "your secret life continues— tonight."

"Yes, with one difference. I don't think anymore that night time is a time for spying. It isn't necessary; it's a time when secrets can be had just for the asking, given as freely as confessionals to a priest."

"Who are these confessers?" asked Paul.

"They're everyone, everywhere. Usually I stay here till four or five, then I go out to a café and talk to strangers. Those are the opposite, the witching hours—four and five—when all defenses are down."

"What people tell you with their defenses down isn't always true."

"I don't care about the truth. I want their stories—the words that possess them. I ask them to tell me their stories. I don't interrupt, I don't give advice. That's what surprises them and opens them up further: that I want only to listen and be possessed by them." As she spoke, she swayed gently on the divan; she was fading in and out of his consciousness.

"And your informants—do they all become your lovers?"

She got up and walked to the bed where he lay, bent over him, kissed him on the lips, and ran her hand gently down the length of his arm, stroking each of his fingers in turn. "What are you thinking about? That all my informants are men, and I need them to make love to me? I want their stories. And stories aren't about things that have happened. They're the inventions of moods. And when you go to women to learn about moods, you never come back empty-handed."

"Never?"

"I'll tell you which women it's always true of: women in pain, women without a chance of *not* being harmed, women who've fallen from social grace—your social grace. The more they suffer, the more they come to feel something tenderer and more nuanced than your common masculine bullying and re-sentment."

"Whom are you thinking of?"

"Lonely women without luck or education: old women, lost and forgotten, with bags full of scavengings; prostitutes, their makeup running, battered, outraged but too amazed to go to bed, wanting to stay up longer. Young girls, strays, without a chance . . . ."

"So you're not just a listener: you hear and you judge."

She looked at him closely.

"You think that women are truer to their feelings, and you don't keep this secret from the women you listen to. You try to help them with this idea against men."

"No, not a lot—not often."

"You like the stories these women tell you better than those men tell you."

"Men lie more."

Paul watched her warily.

"I've often met men who've lied," she said. "I don't mean to take away from their distress. But the elements of the game seem to be: one, a man is distressed; two, he lies; three, he finds relief in getting me to believe his lie."

"He knows you know he's lying. Your complicity excuses the lie."

"I don't agree." She seemed to have withdrawn to a point where she was less remote than proud, hard, and self-indulgent. One could find in her an only contrived and insub-stantial relief, because there really wasn't in her the will to help, just the desire to know—whether the truth or stories, it didn't matter. The grace one got was just an accident of her curiosity.

Suddenly the whole elaborate decor seemed part of her hardness, her design to make him tell his story. The white kimono, her clear voice, the pale silk hangings were the glue of a spider's web, and he could be caught in this viscous tangle of cleverness and greed. He kept calm and said, "You know, you're something of a parasite, you feed on others' misery— their wounds, their squalor. You call them stories, and you come away sleek and beautiful." He began to regret the adventure, and he conjured at the margins of consciousness the other woman whom it would cost him forever.

Marguerite got up fast, her white silk swirling around her, and laughed: not friendly, not unfriendly, full-throated, whole-hearted. She laughed again and she really was laughing, not playing a part.

"What's so funny?" Paul had to quell a melodramatic impulse to scowl at her.

"Wait—I'm not laughing at you, Robert, I'm laughing at myself, at the truth that's been told and glad you found it out." She looked for a minute as if she were treasuring him. Her moods were worrying. She kept her distance.

She began to glide around the room, talking about the nourishment that stories gave you—stroking objects and smoothing her hair in the mirror. She wanted to know if he were feeling nourished. "Come on, Robert, your being displeased doesn't frighten me, but it doesn't make it any easier to talk. Robert, smile!"

The repetitions of the name disheartened him. If she was a voyeur—indeed one twice removed from her object, her glance always fixed on herself, as she watched him—what was he? He was her object, "it" for the night in a game of her invention, which borrowed its rules from the hidden life of the victim. But in what way was he different from her? He too was watching everything happen, though not to himself, but to Robert, his own creature. And suddenly he couldn't bear the airlessness anymore, so many mirrors lowered into an abyss: he wanted all masks off.

"You mean Paul," he said. "My name's not Robert; it's Paul." He stood before her, hands clenched and stretched out, but not touching her. "What's yours?" She was smiling a little. "You're not going to say it's Marguerite. I won't believe you."

"Why not?"

"Because it would be too perfect, it would fit too well not to be an invention."

She held her ground. "My name is Marguerite."

"I don't believe you," said Paul.

"It's true. . . . I see, you're waiting for the rest. The truth, without invention—the facts."

"Yes," said Paul.

"All right. My husband's a musician; my daughter goes to the *École bilingue*. You don't want to hear about our apartment in Neuilly, do you? There, you see: there's the truth. I'm not hiding it; it's just that few ever ask me for it."

"Why should I think you're not lying?"

"You don't have to; what does it matter anyway?"

"The truth matters."

"The truth, yes, but not what you call the truth."

"We call the same thing truth. If you kill someone, it's not a story."

"A story could kill. And that's why a story must be watched. And so first it must be heard, and to hear it you must love it. When I call up truth, I don't hate the stories that cling to it."

"That's only another story. What you call stories I call lies."

"I call it a little clarity falling over the past."

"No," said Paul. "Poems that do not tally with their writer's actual life and knowledge are lies."

"Who said that? A man? Well, he was wrong. Lies are subterfuges, told for profit. Poems are pure."

"Pure!" He got up, walked into the living room, and threw himself onto the couch—naked, morose, and growingly conscious of the trouble in store on account of his recklessness. Marguerite's voice came from behind him. "Paul," she said, still very equable, very calm, "what were you trying to achieve when you invented Robert?"

He wanted to leave now, but he strove to be polite. "I was only playing. But something's happened since: the mask has assumed the features of a real person. And when you take on the identity of a real person"—he stopped for a moment—"you've committed plagiarism. You've stolen moral property."

"Marguerite is my own mask—my nighttime mask, always the same. Marguerite goes back to my childhood; I was already Marguerite when Eric was Mathurin."

"Your name's not Marguerite? You borrowed Marguerite from someone? I was right!"

"That doesn't matter. There's no advantage in borrowing it: it's a mask for my freedom."

"That could be true of my mask," said Paul. Just as Marguerite had set out each night to find another story, he had set out to discover more of Robert. As Marguerite had listened to others, so Paul had emptied himself in order to take in the other. There was one big difference—Margot. If he was searching for Robert, it had been at her behest.

The thought hit him hard. He did not understood Margot's motives. He got up and poured himself some brandy. Was his failure of penetration just a matter of intellectual weariness? Then he could not be sure of the answer. He shook his head impatiently; he must find his bearings. He looked around the room as if he were lost in it: it was like the moment suddenly after awakening, when it is urgent to know where you are; and you panic, because, for a second, time and space hitch. The strangeness of the place was making it unseeable; there was nothing to compare it with. He stopped to name his sensations. A lampshade with silk fringes was glimmering in the corner. In a porcelain vase hung two limp birds of paradise.

Marguerite stood in the doorway with her hair drawn back. What did she want? To steal his night, to suck a story out of him. He hated her silken cage. The scene was mawkish, a candy-box stage for amateur theatricals. The woman was mad. Paul felt a huge impatience. He jumped up, spilling his brandy on the cushions: "I'm sorry. I'm not in the mood for your game."

Marguerite was in the bedroom hanging up her clothes. He ran after her. "Are you listening to me?"

"Were you saying something?"

"Are you trying to make me angry?"

"I'm willing to listen to you"—she turned to him—"to any arguments you might have."

"Arguments? Well, what do you say to this one?" He was standing over her: he took hold of her shoulders, pretended to squeeze them hard but did not, then slid his hands down her back and, embracing her, would not let her go. "That is how I refute your solitude. Where is your freedom now?"

She struggled: reaching behind her, she removed his hands and stepped away from him. "It's always possible to strike a book with an axe. You might consider that truth and so part of the game. I consider it the end of the game." She shook her head. "Leave me now, thanks. You'll find your clothes on the chair: the bathroom is over there." She walked out of the room without looking back and closed the door.

Paul strode into the bathroom and looked at his face in the mirror. It was only his face and not his best. He had never before played the bully in a discussion of that sort. As he looked in the mirror again, set into pink marble and surrounded with flowers—more flowers!—he saw burning blotches on his throat and cheeks. Why had he insulted her? She hadn't really harmed him, she'd been calm throughout, but she had been detached. That was the provocation. This was not the same woman who had responded to his lovemaking with excitement and trickiness. The thought of their having lain together, of him inside her, their hands clasping, their mouths together—all that inexpressibly intimate, rhythmic movement was a scandal. Right now she was probably making notes about his behavior in bed and out of it. He was falling under the head of masculine failings, weaknesses—bullying.

He picked up a crystal tumbler sparkling on the marble table and balanced it in his palm. Then, on a sudden impulse, he aimed its heavy base at the mirror and saw the glass of mirror and tumbler explode into a shower of pieces—some dark, some bright. He stared down at glittering bits and splinters on the tub and on the silk rose carpet. He turned to see in the intact glass of the cabinet the disjointed image of himself standing with his arm still raised, as though he were condemned to repeat the act of aiming the glass forever. He saw the ugly gash in the wall which sent out cracks in intriguing senseless lines. He felt pained but justified.

He opened the taps and splashed cold water on his face and neck. And with a sense of purpose he left the bathroom, slowly and deliberately put on his clothes, and walked out of the bedroom without looking back.

The kitchen was close and dark, lit only by a small lamp on

the table where Marguerite sat writing. She had put back on her rimless glasses, and her bright hair was coiled into a knot. Her expression did not change as she glanced up, her black and gold fountain pen poised above a notebook covered with little squares. He asked if he might sit down. She nodded. He pulled out a chair opposite her.

"I broke the bathroom mirror. I don't know why. I'll pay for the damages."

She got up, took a china bowl from the cabinet and poured coffee into it, added steaming milk, and placed it in front of him. Then she walked out of the room.

She returned. "Why did you say that you broke the mirror? The mirror's fine."

Paul looked at her and frowned. He got up. She took him by the elbow to show him: the mirror was intact. The crystal tumbler was in its place.

He walked back into the kitchen and sat down. As he watched her, cupping the bowl in his hands, he believed that she was the right person to tell. Undoubtedly she was honorable, despite her trappings, and she knew the underside of real experience.

"I want to talk to you, but perhaps you don't want to listen to me."

"I'm willing to listen."

"My name is Paul van Pein. I teach history at a university. For a long time now, I've been living at some distance from myself, and the sensation keeps getting stronger. The mirror thing confirms it."

Her eyes were directly on him.

"The first time I became aware of this feeling, I was still a child spending the summer in Paris. My grandmother had arranged a visit to the Bibliothèque nationale to see an exhibit of bibles and illuminated manuscripts. I went with a carefully chosen cicerone, a librarian, who explained every object to me in fastidious detail. As I struggled to pay attention—my grandmother would expect me to recite in the evening everything I had learnt—I saw that I could flee into an other, an adjacent world. With this discovery, which I call 'the second state,' came the idea of joining the two worlds explosively, forcing reality to submit to my fantasy on my terms.

"In my first attempt I pretended the police were after me

and my being a schoolboy was only a disguise. By the end of that summer, my games had become more elaborate. One afternoon, at the Orangerie, I decided that if my guide said the word *nettement* once more, I would throw a screaming fit. She did, and I did. I rolled around on the parquet floors, crying my lungs out, causing a horrible rumpus among the attendants and worrying my grandmother to death."

Marguerite was leaning back in her chair.

"By the time I was in college, these games had become something of a preoccupation. Whenever the hold of reality became too exclusive—meaning, whenever I became bored or depressed—I violently broke it up. Sometimes it was as homely as inventing a nosebleed in the middle of a lecture. I'd wait for the speaker's rhetorical altitudes, then cry out and stagger up and out, stiff-legged, head thrown back, handkerchief in place to staunch the vacant flow. Another time I wrote, and even succeeded in publishing, a pastiche of the work of one of my professors, hoping that he would recognize it. In graduate school, after I'd married, I had in our domesticity and my wife's complaisance a handy stage for improvisation. Restless and disgusted by our puny reality, I could be tirelessly cruel. The result was: her tears, her threats of leaving, my anxiety, and a sort of lovemaking afterward, which we referred to as 'R&R'— reconciliatory rape."

"And so Robert is part of the game—in the absence of domesticity?"

"I'm not playing a game anymore."

"Your wife took revenge on you?"

"We were divorced a long time ago. I haven't seen her for years."

Marguerite looked thoughtful. After a pause she said, "What holds these episodes together in your mind?"

"Each one is a scene I staged—and made others submit to. They seemed like scenes of real behavior, but the intentions behind them were faked."

"Then you changed."

Paul shook his head. "Two years ago I was at work on a manuscript commissioned by a trade publisher, on novels and prostitution in Vienna at the turn of the century. It was meant as Christmas presents for coffee tables and sensibilities of impeccable varnish. The exercise was mechanical, I was bored and impatient. I knew my colleagues were jealous of the money I'd got and disdainful of my writing for trade, but as I'd already proven I could be a scholar and a successful one, I didn't really give a damn. It was the tedium, the bleary, self-important, word-mongering drear, the wrapped up crassness of the university that had me half-mad. Then suddenly I saw my chance. A wild elation filled me. I would show them—and show myself—what I wasn't afraid to make them accept.

"I spent a couple of days searching for the right text—one not too well-known but not too arcane either, and I found it in a volume on the Vienna police by Lew Wandsworth, the English Austrianist, published some years earlier to little fanfare (it had neglected to consider the police *as* the tropes). Anxious to begin my adventure, I took out my chapter on Arthur Schnitzler and, after inserting into it a couple of pages of Wandsworth's text, sent it out to be published in a journal. You know what that's called, don't you?"

"What you called it before: plagiarism."

"Yes, a most expressive word—it sounds like food poisoning. Plagiarism, the act fetishistically proscribed by the academic community."

"That excited you."

"Yes, for over a year, as I finished my book, the knowledge of what I'd done gave my life an edge of danger and a sense of superiority, because I knew something no one else knew and had dared something no one else would dare."

Though Marguerite's face was in shadow, he could still read her expression. It was not sympathetic; it was devoid of even the usual signs of curiosity. If she were silently judging him, that wasn't grounds for him to feel he was lost or being betrayed. He knew that he was entering her in a way that went beyond ordinary attentiveness or a sense of community.

She said quietly, "Why did the editor of a magazine publish a plagiarized article?"

"It came out on the back pages of *Comparative History*—a backwater journal whose editors, like sluices, are so receptive to submissions, they do not care whether the piece is responsible, and reading it is beside the point. If it can be paginated, it is printed."

"Still, you submitted it—why?"

"It had to do with the the intellectual climate, with the smug denial of truth in history writing. I already told you I faked scenes that looked like real behavior."

"I remember."

"Well, critics took this as the normal case. They said that history writing looks intended but is actually a fake. Historians restage other writers' scenes with words they blindly borrow. So I framed the so-called normal case."

A shadow crossed Marguerite's face but she remained composed.

"I can't explain it all to you. But if I were talking to myself, I'd say: 'So history writing's a "wash" of other people's words? Then I'll give you a bath of it.'"

Marguerite said quietly "You were found out?"

"I didn't know that an exposé had appeared in the cult journal *Semioline*. It sent them running, one by one, to Wandsworth's book. One day I received an anonymous note on departmental stationery, which I recognized as the hand of my Chair, informing me that I might be interested in consulting X's piece in journal Y. I found it and felt the glory go: my mood, a sort of peaceful expectancy, drained away. I was scared, bored in advance at the confusion that was about to come, but above all angry with myself at being taken so off guard. It was as if I'd been woken from a dream by the snarling of a dog I'd forgotten I'd leashed to my bed.

"The scandal became public. I tried to limit the damage by explaining myself at the national meeting last Christmas."

"What did you say?"

"That I had committed a textual *acte gratuit*. I begged at least the indulgence in theory of my colleagues, most of whom were professors of that very crime."

"They all plagiarized?"

"I meant that almost everyone was a professor of the theory of the gratuitous text, while no one, of course, *professed* it— or anything else. I was the first in the humanities to plagiarize, in recent times."

"You sound quite proud of your deed."

"There was something timely about it. Remember, my work was good enough, I was above the need to borrow. But I have never let myself get away with it. My defense was only theatrical. The issue was never really one of history writing."

Marguerite looked at him. "What then?"

"Bursting into what's not allowed—something like that— and making it prevail."

"Yet you can't forget your crime."

"Not the crime of doing it—for being so ill-prepared for my exposure. I allowed myself to feel ashamed—and bored."

"You forget about the victim—Wandsworth."

"Victim—or hero? I wrote to him to apologize that I had made of him an unwitting victim of the brain drain. I expected that he would tut-tut it in the disapproving middle-class way. Instead, he wrote a little note saying how flattered he was to have been borrowed by a member of so distinguished a faculty."

"But, of course, it wasn't borrowing. It was theft."

"As I said: it was theft, with a point—a gratuitous act, done for a bigger purpose."

"It was reckless."

"Yes, that's what appealed to me."

"You're a hard-necked sinner."

"I'm suffering all the same. I feel outraged by what has happened, especially at my inability since to live with joy or sense of purpose. The matter is one of truth, you see, and I want to find it out."

"So you've run away."

"Perhaps, but not from them. By the time I decided to come here, I was beyond caring about others' opinions of me. I was angry with myself. I thought if I buried myself in a far-off place, this old Adam would come to light—maybe as a clair-voyant noble savage—and I could shrug off past hesitations once and for all."

"And has old Adam come?" Marguerite was very quiet, not moving from where she sat in the shadow.

"It came. It came for a minute, but then it in turn was taken from me."

"I don't understand you."

Paul was quiet for a moment.

"Ah, you mean this Robert persona. Robert has borrowed you."

"It's not just Robert; it's all of them." (God! Catherine—

and the hours going by; he would never be able to get back to her.) Paul sat motionless, hardly believing how awful he felt and wondering whether he could die of it. He stared at this woman. "Oh damn it, I think it is your fault."

"It is? How, pray?"

"I was supposed to meet someone tonight—a woman. I decided to forget. How could I otherwise? In the middle of our lovemaking—I mean, in the middle of your seduction."

"My dear friend, you're too old to be seduced."

"I know. . . . It was unfortunate."

"There you go again!"

"No, not you, I mean this Robert."

"You speak in riddles."

"There was another Robert in her life—the real one, though she also knew me as Robert."

Marguerite pondered. "She came into your life because you took the name Robert?"

"No. She's better than that. She's only the victim of my tenacity and Robert's pride."

"Your tenacity?"

"In holding on to my Robert mask."

She stared at him. "You know this Robert?"

"I've met him, but he's written me off, though Margot . . . ."

"Margot!"

"Margot is the source of it all. I don't know how to deal with her. The situation gets more intricate every day. What does she want? I don't quite see it. She never wanted me to have anything to do with Catherine, but I've persisted. It's really Robert Margot wants, I know that."

"Why don't you just leave them all to it, just walk away."

"I can't. I want them, there isn't anything I want except them."

Marguerite came out of the shadow and drew closer to him. "That isn't true."

"I'd like to tell you more about it—but I don't see the whole in outline well enough. I have to go further, I have to find out more." He got up. "I'd better go now."

Marguerite gripped his arm. "I don't think you should. You're exhausted. I'll give you something to help you sleep."

Paul looked around. It was half past five. "I didn't know how late it was." He felt her pull him back into a bedroom but not the one in which they had made love. She folded back the covers while he undressed. In bed, the sheets soft against his skin, he reached up to her, "Come on in with me."

"No, you'll sleep better without me," she said. Her lips touched his. "And you'll know what to do better if you wake up alone."

He pulled her down and pressed his cheek against hers. She drew away, smiling. The lights went out, and he was alone.

Chapter Twelve

For five days it had been raining in Draguignan. Paul stood under a chestnut tree in the Place du Marché, the collar of his leather jacket buttoned to the throat, his arms folded against his chest, straining to see through the drizzle. He had been waiting at this spot every afternoon for a week. And now, at last, the Mercedes rolled up, and he saw Robert rush out into the bookstore. After the chill and the strain, the expectation of reward was elating. In this instant his vigil became something real: he had only to stay alert until Robert came out again.

His hair and face were soaking. He had not known it could rain so hard and long in the south of France. The wait had been difficult. At least the bookstore had kept the same afternoon hours as the rest of the shops and opened only at four. On the first day he'd gone inside and browsed for an hour, immersing himself in the *I Ching*, which warned against irritable strangers. But every time the door bell jingled, the nerves at the back of his neck had jumped. Then he'd decided he did not want to be taken by surprise. So he had either stood in the opposite corner of the old square or wandered once again around it, peering into windows at dusty, ill-assorted displays of shoes, radios, and shampoos, rehearsing what he would say when Robert turned up. Now Robert was here.

The first thing, if their meeting was to be a success, was to know exactly what he wanted to happen. But this was difficult, since only the meeting itself would give him his cues. He knew what their relation must finally do: it must justify his stay at La Casaubade. With that result in hand, he would have a new beginning, an embryonic formula for the future. Robert would be more than just the substance of the meetings that would occupy the next months. With Robert he would achieve a view on his future. Margot had attributed such powers to him, and she was not given to idle praise.

Paul knew that his plan was a little mad and hopeless: how could another put him to rights? And yet he could not put out of his mind her vision of Robert as sage. Furthermore, it would be wrong to rule out the possibility that he, Paul, had lost the thread. It was only common sense to accept another's help.

He looked at his watch, then got under the awning of the drugstore next to Lo Pais, glancing into one of the windows and returning to a large cardboard photograph advertising face cream. This was new: he registered its novelty with a sinking feeling. It was Catherine—his lover for a night had evidently modeled for Lancôme. The memory of her naked belly disproved the knowledge that she'd driven him from her apartment. He saw her now as she'd faced him, icy and constrained. He'd come into the hall and waited for her to finish answering the telephone. He stared at her; she did not want him to watch her, but he could not risk letting his eyes stray. He desperately wanted things between them to be different, and he almost felt he could achieve this change by staring intensely at her. If she would not relent, at least he would not allow her to increase her advantage.

It was an ordeal but unavoidable. He would not be satisfied with his memories of her body: the loss he'd felt on waking alone had included Catherine's knowledge of Robert and Margot. It was something he had to try for even in his shattered state. After Catherine laid down the receiver, he began to apologize, at first in a sort of threatening sing-song until, impatient at his own hesitation, he fought to find his voice. She acted as if she were being asked, much against her will, to overhear him speak. Then the words came to him, bright and full, rhythmically counterposing antithetical positions, shaping an apologia. The life of the feelings, he said, had to collide with the

the requirements of civility and with the sense of responsibility that dream-like intrusions could sometimes dissipate.

Catherine began to stare at him.

Paul smiled. "Our susceptibility to living fictions," he said, "is a principle of sanity equivalent to the salt of common sense in practical types."

She smiled.

Paul felt encouraged. Such interventions, he explained, while compelling in the moment, had no staying power; and where there was basic, decent friendship, as between Catherine and himself, such distractions could be passed over and forgotten. The two of them stood together on the verge of a discovery. He was speaking of the very life that rose up in his speech. He reached for her hands, saying, "Catherine, do you understand me?"

"Perfectly," she said. "You're a con man."

She said *vous*. How brusque and how bitter—they had lain together a whole night. But he could not stop to take offense; he went on enriching his argument, not letting his panic in.

"That's enough," she said.

"Don't interrupt me now. I just want you to listen to me. I don't expect you to forgive me, only admit that what I'm saying has a certain truth."

"I can't. It doesn't."

"Could you please not be righteously indignant just for a minute," said Paul. And he whispered: "You might learn something."

Catherine shouted: "You're lowly and mean-spirited! I want you out!" And she began pushing him back against the door.

"Catherine . . . ."

"Go away."

"Hear me out."

"No! I didn't let you come to listen to your excuses. I had something to say to you. But now I don't even want to." She was hitting him with her open hands in order to force him toward the door. "Words, words. You think if you say the words right, you'll get me to forgive you, but, no, your words are only as truthful as you are. You're an emotional terrorist— no, not even that, just an actor, aimless and uncaring. It's pulp fiction of the sort you write that nurtures a life without responsibility or shame. Now get out."

At the landing Paul stared at her admiringly; he must act precisely. "My extremity exceeds my sense of shame."

She shook her head.

"I've exchanged my responsibilities—not forgotten them."

Catherine bowed her head angrily and shook it, as she tried to close the door.

"Catherine, listen to me, that night changed everything, forever." He didn't want to go on. He whirled and strode down stairs. The damned thing was that everything he'd said was true.

His body tense, now, he moved forward. Robert was coming out of the store, holding a package of books under the flap of his raincoat. He was moving quickly toward the car. Paul ran toward him. There was no longer time to deliberate a strategy. "Robert, what a surprise!"

Robert looked up from his car door as he heard the voice. "Oh, it's you," he said. "Hello." And he continued to open the door.

"Let's take advantage of the coincidence. I have a lot to talk to you about. Can we have a coffee or a beer somewhere?"

"I'm afraid I don't have time," said Robert. He threw his parcel onto the back seat and got into the car. "Anyway, our last conversation was conclusive from my point of view." He turned the key in the ignition. "Excuse me."

Robert started to turn the car around on the awkward slope where he'd parked, and as he did so, Paul ran for the 4CV, started it, and took off in pursuit of the Mercedes. They sped down the narrow streets, past the statue of the dragon— emblem of Draguignan—and on up a steep winding road leading to the vineyards behind the city, shifting gears, turning at bad angles on the muddy roads, avoiding the small commerical vans sailing around the bends on two wheels. The Mercedes glided along the slick as if attached to it: Paul had never driven the 4CV so fast before, but his will to keep up was imperious.

They were heading past Bargemon up into the next sector of hills behind the town, back into isolated country, and still the Mercedes kept on. By now the rain was pouring down, and he could see the car ahead of him only through the sweeping wipers. Tail–lights burned suddenly in the fog. Paul just had time to brake: he skidded, veering left, then right, then shot forward on a wet patch and with a sickening clatter of tin and glass smashed into the rear of the stopped Mercedes. A shower of fine dust rained down on him; a pale orange light went on around him; he had the anxious and exhilarated sense that when the light went out he would be dead. Instead he woke into the consciousness of what he'd done. His eye and nose hurt badly. And Robert? Paul got out and staggered to the other car. Robert was already coming toward him. Only one of the tail-lights of the Mercedes was burning red, and smoke from the exhaust was spiraling up through the rain.

Robert grabbed him by the shoulders and, staggering, pushed him onto the field next to the road. Paul stumbled but Robert stopped him from falling. He held onto his collar and thrust his face into his. "What the fuck were you following me for?"

Paul cleared his throat. "For her."

Robert glared at him and began choking. "Her! Who the hell is her? Margot?"

Paul nodded.

"Margot!" The tone was incredulous. "I'm still supposed to hear about her," he raged, "from you?" His fist came up from below and slammed Paul on the cheek. Another fist hit his eye. Robert was driving blows at him. Paul covered his face, he was falling, he was on his knees in the mud. Robert turned away, choking on obscenities. Otherwise the night was silent.

Paul began to get up. His face was smeared with water or blood; one of his eyes was closed.

Robert helped him. "Here, get up. I'm sorry, I'm really sorry. Are you all right?"

Paul nodded.

"You'd better get into your car."

They went on over. Paul leaned against the fender; Robert struggled to find a handkerchief. "Here," he said, "wipe your face." Paul took it. "You want to know all about Catherine? Is that it?"

Paul was quiet. He was being rewarded for all his pain and hardship.

"A better person than Margot—a painter, a good painter. You write to Margot? Ask her how she treated Catherine after they became friends. Oh Christ, look at you! How could you have let her get me to hit you? You're a bloody fool." Robert stood gaping down on him without seeing, his eyes shining. "I can't blame you, I can't get away from her. I'm no better than you."

"The horrible nights."

Robert glared at him. He turned away. "A rotten game. Everyone but me, a different dog every night. And she came back to tell me all about it."

He turned and walked a little way off. His voice was calmer. "Catherine helped. She almost got me over it. But Margot wasn't going to let me. She wanted Catherine too—all her Catherines!"

He was wandering around, sputtering to himself; Paul heard the squelch of his shoes in the mud. "Catherine thought Margot was good for maturity, for complexity, that she'd be good for us in the long run. And the result? Catherine ran away. She did, I didn't. She's married now. Think of that. A man came along and took her to Iceland. She was in Iceland the whole time I thought she was dead."

"I'm sorry," muttered Paul.

Robert seemed not to be listening. "That was Margot's doing: she never wanted her, she wanted me to suffer." Robert began kicking the fender of his car back away from the wheel. "But I've paid her back. I've kept her in the dark. She thinks she killed the girl, and so she might have, but she didn't. She's thought the whole time Catherine's dead, and she's been running scared."

Robert was deluded. No one was running scared. The dead woman on the *berges* had turned out to be the carcass of a sick doe.

Robert was shouting, "Or did you ruin that too—you meddler?"

Paul was silent.

"Oh, what's the use."

Paul muttered, "Why do you stay on here?"

"Yes—why? Because I'm still waiting, in case she wants to let me back in, just one more time. What a disgrace. Yes, horrible, it never ends, I can't forget. Maybe someone else will end it for me. Maybe you will." Robert stared at him. "Yes, you. Become Margot's beau, her one and only." He laughed. "I'm sorry. Get away now, go home. Pull yourself together and go home." Robert helped him to get inside. "Come on, start your car."

Paul muttered. "You said, the nights, the horror. You meant New Hebrides."

"Oh shit." Robert let him go.

"You can tell me."

"Are you crazy? You haven't heard anything I said."

"Tell me."

Now Robert was shouting. "Tell you? I told you, once and for all, let things alone," and he turned and stamped back to his car, cursing. Then he climbed in and turned the key. The car groaned, then started. A powerful rush of fumes blew at him. The Mercedes spun for a second, then lurched off.

Paul watched the lights of the car dwindle down the road. He sat for a long time. It had stopped raining. In the twilight he saw the dull silvery flatness of the field and the wide apricot band above the hills. He climbed out into the field and walked in a circle, then got back in the car. He hated the clumsiness of his muddied shoes. He dangled his feet outside and tried to pull off his shoes: his fingers were cold and numb; he couldn't open the laces.

From the inside he pulled the door closed angrily. The key, for example—where was the key? He opened the door to look for it in the mud and then, hurling himself back into the car, from the corner of his eye saw it dangling in the ignition. He turned it. The engine started. He drove down the long sloping hill, warning himself to keep his eyes on the road and watch every detail of the slick surface.

It was dark when he got to La Casaubade. The house looked altogether someone else's. He walked reluctantly across the terrace to the kitchen door. With the lights on, the place was less forbidding. He went up the stairs, looked in the mirror, and, shocked, undressed and turned on the shower. The water stung his face but did it good. He watched the brown rivulets spilling down his body, down his legs—growing paler and paler until they disappeared down the drain, leaving their

sandy sediment on the gleaming porcelain. He let the heat
numb his stinging bruises. When there was no more hot water,
he got out and, standing before the mirror, put iodine on his
cuts and vaseline on the bumps, remembering the evening he'd
come home beaten up by the Sicilian delivery boy: on rounding
the corner, he had walked into the tough who jeered at his
leggings and called him a fag. Paul put his angry face into his
and got a punch in the eye, and then to his permanent shame,
he twisted away and ran home to his mother. She scolded him,
saying, if you must fight, win, but then with tears in her eyes
began to wash his cuts and dab at them.

He pulled on a robe and staggered downstairs, flicking on
the lights. The room was silent. He poured himself a whisky,
and on the first taste of it, he felt a rich thought begin to make
its way through him. The telephone rang, shatteringly. He
rushed into the living room to answer it.

"Paul," said Jean, "have you been away? I've called you at
least four times. We had friends from India I wanted you to
meet."

"I was in Paris."

"What a good idea. Was it splendid?"

"I saw Catherine."

"I'm so glad! How did it go?"

"It was awful."

"Come on, it can't have been that bad."

"It was awful."

Jean was silent for a moment. "Why don't you come and
have supper with us."

"I can't."

"You can't? But we're having eggplant. You love eggplant."

"Normally I do."

"Is there something the matter with your voice?"

Paul was silent.

"Well, if you change your mind and want to talk, do
call back."

"Yes."

"Well, goodbye."

As Jean hung up, Paul stood holding the receiver, thinking
that one of the things he could have said to him was he was
desperate for their kindness. But he could not tell him what

was also true, that they would only muffle what crucially mattered.

So he raised the glass to his lips and took a long swallow. "Catherine," he whispered out loud, wonderingly, "Catherine." She hadn't been the one at all. Robert's Catherine was in Iceland with a new husband, and his Catherine, who was she? As the truth started to spread through him, her image grew brilliant for an instant in its separateness and then palpably began to fade. He wanted her to grow strong and independent of the others, but she refused. Catherine vivid and angry in her room in Paris was vanishing outside their orbit. He had nothing but his sentiment of an obscure trinity weighing on his world—and their world beyond his reach.

He splashed whisky into the glass.

He had been used. He must have known it all along. But what in the relationship of Robert and Margot had so needed him as go-between? He had played his role to perfection, had even manipulated the evidence himself so that Catherine would draw him into it more deeply. Was that why he'd been beaten up? He should have waited and been more prudent, damn it, before making love to her in Margot's bed. Their sleeping together was not so much a grave moral conundrum as a matter of common sense.

"All right, Margot, it's between the two of us now." He said this to the stone walls, soaring into shadow at the top of the house.

He was hungry. It made him happy to be hungry because it was a sign of health. In the kitchen, he bit into a heel of bread and cut some *chèvre*, but the knife slipped from his hand and gashed the soft part of the palm between the thumb and the forefinger. He stuck his hand in his mouth, then held it out. The blood dripped onto the cheese and the board; he stopped, struck by its extreme dark redness against the faintly greenish chalk-white of the cheese. How long would it take for her life blood to drip away, and how would it feel, the slow ebbing of her strength? Would her thoughts begin to blur as though their edges had been erased? Would the tearing anguish simply fade, or would she be overwhelmed by one great fear? He roused himself and sucked his palm and went for some gauze from the medicine shelf.

There was a rustle behind him, on both sides, and as he

turned, not too startled, they were there around him—the rag-
tag gang that had passed him on the road that night at Varda's.
They stood quietly, more amused than hostile, seeming to
await his reaction. There was a great theatricality in their arrested movement; only the dirty, multicolored folds of the
women's skirts still swayed from the stealth and speed with
which they'd entered. Nearest him stood a scrawny figure in
loose pantaloons, with only a scrap of shirt on, a rag of
washed-out mauve around his neck, a tangled mass of hair and
eyes of the same greenish-yellow color, staring at him, expectant, exhilarated. Behind him two women were posing, mock-
ing and provocative in their sagging postures: the one with
lank green hair, pasty skin, red eyes that glinted like a parrot's;
the other with gypsy colors, red lips, gold earrings, and a dirty
bandage around her calf. The kitchen and the living room were
ignited with these figures, a dozen of them, waiting for him to
begin their crazy game.

Slowly, from the raised kitchen floor, aware of their eyes
fixed on his every movement, Paul raised his glass: "Welcome,"
he said. "Welcome to the magic circle." He stared at the gypsy
woman. "You've come to play?"

She smiled faintly.

"A toast," said Paul.

They waited.

It came to him. The players are here, he thought. "To
Margot," he cried, "to Margot—our dramaturge."

They mouthed the words and laughed.

He held up his glass. "To the *démon du Midi*."

They seemed to like that.

"Come on," Paul shouted, "have something to drink. I'm
glad you came."

Paul thrust glasses from the shelves into their hands and
began pouring and pouring, urging them to take things, pushing toward them bread, cheese, apples, jars of nuts and olives.
And as he talked, they talked, in a growing riot of cries, laughter, barking dogs, bottles popping, nuts being cracked, knives
hacking, plates scraping, pits being spat out against the walls,
onto the floor.

"Yes, yes," said Paul. "I've been waiting for this."

A lanky fellow with wispy red hair, broken nose and dirty

fingernails, his shirt a sort of gray felt waistcoat covered with bottle caps and tin logos, put his tattooed arm around Paul's shoulders and bawled to the others in Kidderminster English: "It's a brother-poet we have here. Be nice to him: he speaks in tongues. What's your name, brother?" He turned his slate-colored eyes to Paul.

"Paul—and Robert too!"

"Let's drink to Paul—and Robert too!"

As they roared back, "To Paul—and Robert too!" the blowsy girl in the living room ripped open a pillow from the couch and threw it into the air, and they all stopped for a moment, Paul included, to watch the feathers pour out of the bright silk rag and descend in a cloud.

Now a woman with curly hair and a rose-colored bridesmaid's dress glided up next to him. "It's beautiful, isn't it?" she whispered.

Paul said, "Are you American?"

"Yes, but there are only two of us. The others are from Europe—England, Germany, Belgium, and one from Hungary. We represent the corrupt Western countries."

"I see, you're idealists."

She looked delighted. Her face was turned up to him. A look of innocence shone from it, and he was struck with admiration. "Why is your face so sore?" she said.

"A run-in with a friend."

"Now, girl, what are you doing, monopolizing our host?" It was the gypsy who rudely thrust herself between the two of them. "Get us some more to drink, birdie."

A Bach cantata was blaring, and with the gypsy's arms around his waist, Paul swayed and staggered.

"Here, take a drag." It was the slate-eyed fellow again, and Paul dragged deeply and held the smoke in his lungs, then dragged again, and laughed aloud with pleasure. His senses had never felt so acute, never had his reason cooperated with his desires so perfectly in heightening his sense of life. He tightened his arms around the woman and felt her soft breasts crush against him, the nipples hard, before she limped away.

"Catch me." And she was lost in the wild mob. Now the walls were quick and throbbed with life. Music pounded in all the corners; shadows leapt and faded in the sweet, heady haze of reefers and guttering candle flames. Paul stopped at the sight of the fire. Everything was the color of pink and flame—the fire, Courbet's *The Winnower*, and the lamps on the pink exposed stones. Two women were roasting sausages—on what, for a fuel? On Margot's letters, they'd found her letters, they were twisting them into faggots and cooking pork with them. Paul staggered: it was thrilling—horribly thrilling, but there it was, it was being done, he saw it, and it was no worse than it was: just horrible, in its way, as if he'd seen Jen fucked by her Paraguayan lover. He shivered: he was being touched and kissed and stroked by the others as they moved confusedly around him—laughing, shouting, smoking, drinking, eating, pulling him along in their discovery of the rooms, rolling on the beds, running their hands and bodies over Margot's surfaces, snatching and playing with her fur rugs, covers, cushions— singing, chanting; it was as if her house were alive again with the patterns of an old, a wild and fabulous ritual of devastation. And on the stairs he felt again the push of warm breasts and the acrid breath of the gypsy woman as she reached down through his robe, arousing him, before disappearing into the crowd that tramped by on its way downstairs again.

As they moved around him, he became aware of the silence, and turning into the living room, he saw the bronze god, standing on a chair, his armored waistcoat gleaming, reaching for the tapestry, a knife heavy in his hand.

"Yes," he shouted, "it wants my knife!"

All faces were lifted up to his. Someone cried out, "Yes," and then another and then others: "Yes," they cried, beginning to clap their hands and stamp and shriek, "yes, it wants his knife." The young god laughed out loud. He held up his hand. There was silence again.

"So be it. We shall do as you say, I and our host the poet Paul—and Robert, too. Comrades, you have heard him: he is one of us. Bring him forward!" Paul felt hands urging him toward the tapestry, and he was tugged and pushed and hauled up onto their shoulders. The bronze god held hard onto one of his hands, while from below a knife hilt was thrust into the other. And as Paul swayed toward the thick, faded, silken folds of the tapestry, the other intoned, "Free us from the bonds of Europe," and raising the blade, he gestured for Paul to do the same with his.

The hilt shaky and slippery in his hand, he felt the steel prick up and rip the first threads, and looking into the slate-colored eyes, he pulled the knife down with all his strength as the others roared their approval and his face twisted with pain.

A chaotic wailing now broke loose with the flash and sputter of wrecked glassware, the B-minor Mass throbbing and soaring, untouched by the violence that raged like fire through the old *mas*. Tables were being hacked with machetes, chairs kicked and splintered, glasses shattered, metal appliances crushed. And he, sometimes leading, sometimes following, thrust his knife along with them—the rubber hilt now hard in his hand as it picked and stabbed its way across familiar surfaces—smashing with every thrust the care and pleasure he had felt for her taste and sensibility.

They were in the bedroom, the room stifling with the press of bodies. He watched in a kind of faint as they pulled his things from cupboards and drawers, heard the breaking of bottles hurled into the bathroom, and felt again the body of the gypsy woman close to his, while over her shoulder he saw the bronze god leaning against the window ledge, his slate eyes watching.

"You want me, don't you," she hissed, fingering him, her lips touching his ear, her pelvis thrust out, pressing against his thighs.

"Yeah," he croaked, unaware of anything but her thick lips and her floppy belly.

Spread-eagled across the bed, his brain registered "Margot's bed," and as he mouthed the words, she tore open his robe with her teeth. His body was convulsed, wave upon wave of excitement swept over him, carried along by the clapping, laughing, shouting mob. Her strong thighs straddling his hips, his hands grabbing hold of her swinging breasts, he watched the ceiling gyrate with sickening speed.

Chapter Thirteen

The nerves in his temples burned like electric wires. He pressed his palms against his cheeks, but the clamminess repulsed him. His cut hand ached: he had to stop the pain. He sat up, stiffened his legs, raised his knees, flung out his hands, grasping at air. He curled up on his side, lay on his back, pressed his soles together—nothing helped. Finally, he opened his eyes to tiny, painful slits and cupped them with his hands against the startling light.

He hoped he would not be sick—that would be decisive proof of his being in trouble—but then he had to run in one lurch to the toilet bowl, where he stood retching, staring with amazement at the salmon-colored stuff that came out of him. Tears stung his cheeks, but the worst pain was gone. He stood up, feeling light-headed, beginning to shake all over—that worried him, and then he found himself back on the bed, grabbing for the sheets and shivering all over again under a wave of nausea. He rushed back to the bathroom, until he was empty even of bile, and there was only dry retching and chills. He got back to bed, rolled the blanket around him, clutched a pillow to his chest, and fell through into darkness.

He woke to see the curtains hanging in shreds; the drawers of the chest were on the floor, his clothing strewn about. The rugs lay matted and stained on the tile floor that still shone from the futile zeal of Madame Onafaro, reflecting in flashes the sunlight that angled in through the shuttered window. Beyond the bathroom door, he could see shattered glass, pills on the floor, creams stopped in their flow, like cooled lava, and a jumble of bloodied towels.

He stepped over the debris and got to the bathroom sink. His drinking glass lay in splinters in the bowl; he cupped his hands under the faucet and drank, his hands numb under the icy water. The lapels of his robe were drenched. He pulled it off, stumbled into the bedroom, and, searching through piles of soiled clothing, found a sweatshirt and the pants to his suit, all the time shutting and opening his eyes to fight against the sensation that the bone around them was being etched away by the light.

He had to negotiate the steps. Feeling his way—his shoulder scraping against the wall and his palms pressed against the banister—he got to the second-floor landing and clutched the iron railing, greasy from his visitors. To the right, the hills awaited him, whiplines clear and flanks on fire. He looked down.

Margot's magic circle!

Smoke furled its way up the darkened stones. The fire had risen so high that the wood frame of the fireplace, whose carved beams followed the incrustation in the stones, had been charred and still was smoldering. Half in the fire, now dead, hung the remains of one of the Moroccan rugs, its blue and magenta scorched. The dining room table was up-ended and the chairs splintered; pieces of their legs lay flung about, while the lamps spewed out their inner cords. The terra-cotta floor was dusted with down from the ripped pillows of the sofa and armchairs, shifting with each breath from the open doors.

Outside, the hills stood unchanged in the clarity of their lines.

He had *exploded* his solitude.

He lurched down the rest of the stairs, through the fouled kitchen, until he was outside. Now he could breathe, and he gulped in the fresh, crisp, wintry air from the terrace of a world that was just beginning all over again. Trees, hedges, and stones stood splendid in their colors and distinctive in their forms, rooted in the day that chattered quietly to itself, long set upon its busy course. And as he stood rocking, he felt again an answer leap up within him—there, on the verge of being.

His eyes moved up to trace the ellipses of a hawk, and he realized that the pain had gone, though the nausea was still deep and might stay a while in the pregnancy of shame. The hawk hung for a second, motionless, in the lucid sky, then dove and disappeared below the world. His eyes followed the lines of the hills; then he turned around again. The house was there, the most nearly perfect of all houses—worth ruining.

The sound of a motor startled him. He turned toward it, not wanting to, and stumbled on a clump of weeds in the gravel, then recovered and stood still. Who had found him out? The police! They would be coming back to question him. They had known he was bluffing when he said he hadn't seen the thugs on the road that night.

He darted back into the house, locking first the kitchen door, then moving swiftly to the living room, where he closed the doors and searched for the keys in the flowerpot. There were no curtains he could draw; they could see in through the panes of the French doors.

He started to straighten things up, smiling at the thought of what remained to be done in two minutes and would require a sorcerer's army of movers, sweepers, carpenters, polishers, and washers-up to set to rights.

There was a crunch on the stones. He moved into the kitchen and, standing in the shadow out of sight, looked out. On his terrace stood a man and woman, both in violet-and-black nylon checkered trousers, with two children, in matching parkas. The man was grunting, calculating the cost of a set-up like this, and concluding that he, for one, would not pay it— too isolated, up here in the middle of nowhere, terrible in winter though not a bad spot for a picnic in summer. No, they couldn't, the woman said, the place was being lived in.

The boy, meanwhile, kicking stones, had steadily advanced toward the house. He was standing next to the first of the living room doors, peering in, cupping his hand over his eyes—while his parents continued to talk and his sister sat with her legs hanging over the edge of the *berge*, kicking at the artichokes. The boy moved on to the next door and stood still, looking in. What the devil could he see, what would he say? Paul craned his neck, studying the lanky figure—knobble-kneed, sandy-haired—his absorption obvious in the tension of his stance, visible to no one but Paul, hidden in the dark of the midden. And then the boy was at the kitchen door. Paul could not move, he could see only the small rectangle of shadow. Suddenly his own face was clear in the light as the boy pushed against the door, hands spread flat, having seen him. All at once—wanting to see the boy's eyes, to register the shock that must be in them—Paul stepped toward the door and stood facing his opponent through the glass, watching as the boy jerked backward. Then Paul stopped, and the two of them looked at each other. Paul nodded a little and smiled into eyes that weren't simple.

"Come on, Paul. What are you looking at? Is anyone there?"

Paul felt stabbed. He put his finger to his lips.

Young Paul turned his head toward the others. "There's nobody, I'm coming." Then he loitered for a moment and turned and looked at Paul. "I have to do something."

"We'll wait for you in the car. We're not having the picnic up here."

The boy turned his face back to Paul, and as he looked into his face, unzipped his pants, took out his penis, and directed the stream against the door of La Casaubade. Paul stood still, arrested by the peculiar silence with which the crime was being committed. With a sideward glance at Paul, the boy tucked his penis back into his jeans, pulled the zipper up, and walked away.

He would not have dared. "The second state" hadn't been vicious; it had been a subterfuge, allowing him to defuse criminal feelings without commiting crimes.

But the comparison was idle. Of what concern to him was his past now—the peaking and waning of his desire to find release in theatrics? History was not discovered by reflection: it's when your life changes only because somebody dies. Reflection, too, would have an end. In his new environment—dark and mazy, green and deep—his language would not be understood, and he'd soon forget the things he once needed to figure out.

He kicked open the door and stared briefly at the wet stain; it meant nothing human. None of them did now, including all their doubles; soon they would no longer have any access to him. He had to make preparations. There must be no sign of life at the house, no trace of anything untoward. Jules must be kept ignorant until he could be out of there. It was only a matter of doing things in sequence.

He started the car and drove it further up the road into a wild rosemary hedge at the tip of the *berge*. He got out, put the gear in neutral, and released the handbrake. Hearing the crash, he walked down to the house, plucking at the feathers that still clung to the sleeve of his sweatshirt; it lacked only the tar. His hand looked waxen in the sun and was the color of Borax soap. A few months earlier, it had been ruddy and strong, but that had been a fake. Provençal gardening! He turned and went through the kitchen and up the stairs to the study.

The printer was twisted but not wrecked. He remembered having seen the Compaq hurled against the wall, but it might have been protected by its case. He pulled the bed aside, retrieved the computer, and then screwed the little cables of the printer into place. He plugged it into the transformer, upside down next to the socket, shoving aside the jumble of books, manuscripts, letters, bills, and draftsman's pencils. He found the box of perforated computer paper that had been kicked behind the chest. Carefully, he inserted a disk into the machine and turned it on. The hum and sequence of clicks and beeps were familiar and soothing: he had liked sitting in front of his machine, readying to write; and he remembered the exhilaration with which he'd sat, months—years?—ago, copying out the lines from Wandsworth, his pleasure peaking with each keystroke. Had he known where that moment would lead, would he have stopped, torn up the pages, and returned to his own work, whose superiority to Wandsworth's had never been in question? What difference would the answer make now? He was on his own: the game was over, he had nothing to borrow, he had to invent out of whole cloth, with nothing and nobody to intervene. You are the task, no master near or far.

With the first, it was easy to maintain the exhilaration.

> Advertising Editor
> *The International Herald-Tribune*
> 23, avenue rue de l'Opéra
> Paris 1er

Dear Sir:

Please publish and bill to me the following advertisement:

> Cottage to let—perfect condition, Upper Wield, in
> Hampshire. Character, charm, newly renovated—
> all mod cons. Terms most advantageous to young
> scholar—woman preferred but gentleman may
> apply.

Thank you for your consideration.

> Yours sincerely,
> Margot Stevens.

Next:

Dear Dut,

I have decided to resign from the university. My reasons
are purely personal, and I hope that my decision will not prove
inconvenient for the Department.

Since I won't be returning, you can take all the books from
my office and put them in the lounge for general distribution. As
for my files, please dispose of them at your discretion. Erase my
hard disk (you just format it).

At this moment I can hardly believe that we have been
colleagues for almost ten years. May I say that you have been an
exemplary upholder of other men's rules, reinvented by your
own timidity? Lacking character you craved a system, never
realizing that the one you administered, with its gaps and ineq-
uities, was a legal dummy of your own ineffectual person.

Would you, therefore, on receipt of this letter, roll it into a
reed, bring it to a point, and stick it up your ass? Thanks. Come
to think of it, this is the first note to you which I shall not have
the duty of signing All the best.

He scribbled his name at the bottom of the sheet and put it into an envelope. On the way down he would leave the letters in the mailbox with a note to the postman to ask Varda for postage.

He had come to the end of his sequence. He drew up another blank screen on the computer.

Dear Margot,

I am writing this letter but not as your tenant. I am returning the obligations that come with your house. My tenure is over. I hope I have learnt my lessons well. The frenzies of your past will not protect you now.

Paul van Pein

And went downstairs to wait for the taxi.

Chapter Fourteen

She sat in front of the fire, rubbing her hands together. The clamminess and cold had got through even the foot-thick walls and now seemed to be slowly turning around her. It had been like this for days—she could not get warm; and ever since she'd received Jean's letter, the image of La Casaubade had gone on tormenting her, adding leaden woe to winter. It seemed now, as if with the destruction of the house, she had also been dispossessed of Robert and would never see either of them again.

What was that sound? A car? She did not want to find out.

Bending over from the leather stool, she poked the fire with her iron and watched the crumbling pine logs fall and blaze up again. She thought of putting her hand into the flames, to scorch it and with a flash of pain distract her from the sullen cold.

There was a knocking at the door. She knew who it was, and she would not answer. He had become so docile now that she had parried the first strong moves in his pursuit. The thought of their clasping each other again under slack sheets revolted her. And when she had let him know this, he had grown so obviously charmed, so attached, it had made her want to scream. It had been nothing but her nervous idleness, her waiting to see what would happen in France, that had made her start up with him at all.

185

The knocking continued, and she saw him standing in the drizzle in his shabby mackintosh, his moustache dripping, his cheeks ruddy from a day in the fields—hoping, longing, gasping to get in under her skirt. Intimacy! If she could have put up with that from Robert, if she could have just pretended to, she would now be sitting in the light, the sun on her cheeks, her gaze lost in the blue-green bloom of the hills stippled with brown and gray but deep, old, alive. A spasm of longing shook her. My Robert, my Casaubade! She had wrenched Catherine from him, but she had lost him by doing so. Paul van Pein had been the wrong one to send.

Lunging across the room, she picked up the novel she had been reading for the last few days, threw it, and saw the cheap binding blow apart in midair and, on its impact with the base of the wall, disintegrate. She had already read so many novels that winter—false leads, an excitement that changed nothing— and the pain was that they'd once filled her with a practically religious ardor for talents immeasurably greater than her own, but to what use? Just a few days before, she had tried to read Paul's book on whores and novels in turn-of-the-century Vienna. His phrases were smart, no doubt, but what did they amount to? Fear masquerading as cleverness, vacuity under control—the flow marked by another sound like water dripping.

"Control" meant . . . what? You thought you got good results when you applied it to someone else, and you despised someone for being without it. But what value did it have in the one instance that really mattered—when you claimed it for yourself? That was the joke: once you spoke to yourself out of need, you saw that you no longer had any control at all or any further right to assume it.

She rubbed her hands together and noticed the two brownish stains on their backs. Maybe there would be some relief, after all, in growing old. Getting it all over with. Getting the whole stupid misadventure over and done with. Then let it hurry up and come! It had the excitement in it, once again, of something absolutely distinguished that one waited for. This was how she had felt as a girl about the pleasures of her womanhood: she would pace the narrow room they had given her, waiting for excitement, for seduction, amazement, ingratitude, betrayal—whatever would shatter the torpor of her confinement. But now her waiting was not full of the hope of pleasure—it was all for a change she wanted to be over. She was tired and dull, her nerves were blunt. Perhaps a walk—but no, he'd certainly manage to accost her: hawk-eyed Holford, lord of the manor, poacher on her peace, the too eager, smiling, fifty-year-old private man. All the steps now in his belated courtship dance were stylized writhings from his dismay at having been cast out of her bed. He called it love—this farce! How she had longed for it, once—a life of shared courage for ideals passionately held; but now she knew, because she'd loved, one didn't need the presence of the lover, quite the contrary. If she were anywhere else—Fiji, Borneo, Katmandu—he could be with her in the right way. She loved him through her life, in the very living of it, but she hadn't lived according to her knowledge.

Probably a foreign country was what she needed now, a worthwhile difficulty again, far from this riskless civility: to be lost again in unknown cities and unreadable lives. Suddenly she shivered, and the memories of all the vile nights were back again. She was alone, listening to the subdued sounds of voices, of animals, familiar creatures turning horrible with nightfall. Alone in her hut—without lights, without candles, muffled, hot, stinging—alerted to the sounds, straining to hear them, to identify them, garbled by night and so more piercing. And the words muttered on in her mind, words in the night from the nights she had suffered, told words, fragments of old conversations with herself, all of them merging oddly. She had tried to explain to herself why she had let them come to her again and again—to expel the silence of the inhuman, and the disgrace of her loneliness, when she was lost in the dark at the end of the world. But Robert had placed a finger on her lips. No explanations, he said, only say what happened. He was disgusted all the same, she could see that in his mouth as they lay together, but he listened to her and said he understood. They were one person that night, and he kept taking her again and again until dawn. But when he left her, she knew that she did not want him ever again to come back to her, infinitely desirable in her corruption as she had now become. She had told him everything, wanting him to absolve her, and instead, she knew, her nights had now become the prod of his desire—her horror had become his spice. She had had to let him go, because he would never let her alone again. And after that he had been after her—he too—fiercely attentive, courting, and raging.

A knock on the door. She looked at her watch. It couldn't still be Holford. He would have gone on home by now and would have changed for Christmas dinner, dressing for a life that almost didn't exist. There would be the stiff white linen, the heavy candlesticks, the creaking cupboards of mahogany sideboards, and the long halls, unwalked, with its paintings of ships and dogs and forebears, unlooked at, gathering dust, but self-importantly there.

Another knock. She got up, pulling her cardigan around her. Probably a Conservative candidate.

She undid the lock, bracing herself against the cold, and saw standing in the doorway a tall, sandy-haired man with regular features and a tense expression. He was holding a folded newspaper.

"Yes?" she said, frowning, her head to one side.

"Margot Stevens," he said, urgently.

She nodded.

"I have come to rent your cottage."

"I beg your pardon?"

He pointed to the newspaper. "Your ad."

She peered at it. She shivered from the cold. She felt a vague dread.

"May I come in?"

She backed away from the door. He turned to close it, then suddenly he pushed forward into the room, brushing against her so hard that she cowered from the impact. He had surprised her. She thought she was falling and reached for the arm of the couch for support, but he put his arms around her waist, and they fell down together. He lay on top of her, and when she cried out, he pressed his fingers against her mouth and chin, saying, "No, please don't." She struggled until, with his left hand, he took something pointed and metallic out of his raincoat pocket, slipped it up under her sweater and against her ribs, and, crying out, stuck it against her, but no further. His other hand freed her mouth and grasped her wrist, holding it above her head. Even in her amazement she listened. "I only loved you," she heard him say, and then his body relaxed. She struggled free and sat up. She felt him scrambling, then he too suddenly squatted back down. His eyes were brilliant. Hardly apart, they stared into each other's face. He thought he knew her: her eyes were purple, she had a papery smell. "I only came to answer your ad," said Paul, and feeling her slow smile go through him felt so keen a surge of pleasure, he knew he'd go mad if he had to live without it.